There Was a Rainbow After All

We just had to find it

By

Jane K. Parish

A book about the successes, trials and tribulations of a family moving through the aftermath of The Great War (World War I), the peace and prosperity that followed the effects of The Great Depression and the suspense of eight sons facing World War II. The story tells a remarkable tale about one family's tremendous efforts to overcome adversity in the face of great odds.

Poplar Street Press

P.O. Box 560605

Charlotte, NC 28256

(704) 549-0084

E-mail: poplarstpress@bellsouth.net

There Was a Rainbow After All
We just had to find it

Copyright © 2008 by Jane K. Parish

Poplar Street Press

P.O. Box 560605,

Charlotte, NC 28256

Tel: (704) 549-0084

E-mail: poplarstpress@bellsouth.net

This is a work of fiction based on the real lives and experiences of some of the characters in the book. Some names have been changed for artistic reasons only. Others have been retained in order to convey the true flavor of the period.

FIRST EDITION

ISBN – 978-0-615-25441-8

Acknowledgments

This book would not have been possible without the constant support and encouragement of my dear husband, Joe. When my intensity or interest flagged, he was always there with his supportive words of encouragement and challenges to do the work and finish the project. I believe that it takes a kind and tolerant spouse to endure the frustrations of a novice writer and for that to him I am forever grateful.

My heartfelt thanks to David, my high school sweetheart. After fifty years we have become reacquainted. His knowledge, talent and patience helped make the writing of this book possible. I am profoundly grateful.

1

NEB

1915

The steam locomotive spewed a big puff of dirty, dark smoke over the already dirty, dingy little town of Gaston, North Carolina before the troop train came to a complete stop in front of the one room depot.

Neb Kohler, the only person getting off in the town of about 17,000 stepped onto the black tar platform and stared at the depot. The air was hot. The dirty, woolen uniform he was wearing was hot. The train had been hot. It was July. He was miserable. *Should I go inside? What should I do? Where should I go?*

He had been on the train for most of four days as it wound its way across the south. The porter, that had walked up behind him, said, "You look tired, son. Getting off here? You must live close by."

Neb turned and looked at the porter and thought to himself, *I'm not sure where I live or what I'm going to do.* He simply nodded. As if he wasn't already dirty enough, the steam engine puffed out two more clouds of soot and smoke, sounded the loud whistle and began to pull away. The porter jumped back on and Neb was left standing alone on the platform.

He went inside the depot that smelled of wood furniture polish and oily-pine floor cleaner. The room had to be cleaned twice a day in an effort to keep down the grit and grime – a procedure that, obviously, had not worked. He looked around and found a water fountain. He got a long drink, then filled the canteen that had been flung over his shoulder.

He took the canteen when he was discharged from the army post in Texas, where he had been for the past two years. The post was a temporary tent camp set up by the army just outside El Paso and Fort Bliss. He had never really understood why he was there. His unit had not done anything of any significance the entire two years. That was probably because the United States didn't really get into "The Great War" until two years later. A lot of the boys, when they left, took small things. The army didn't care since they no longer had any use for them. But the truth was, the only things Neb owned were the canteen, the miserably hot uniform and the money in his breast pocket that he had saved from his last two pay periods at the post.

As tired as he was, he still stood over six feet tall and his eyes were clear blue. His full lips and dark blond hair only further authenticated his German ancestry.

Until he joined the army, he had lived some 30 miles northeast of Gaston in a small settlement called McLean. Most of the people in the area were poor farmers. Like a lot of small towns in that part of the state, it was named for a person. Now old, Mr. McLean was the first to settle there and owned the most land.

Neb wasn't sure if he still had family there, but he supposed that's where he should go. It was better than spending his precious little bit of money on a cheap room in Gaston. Granted, Gaston was slightly more prosperous than McLean, but it was still a dingy little town. The few times in his life he had visited Gaston, he had never liked it.

It was about noon. If he started walking now and if fatigue didn't take over, he could easily make it half-way to McLean before dark. He slung the canteen over his back and started back out of the depot.

As he walked through the door, a coarse, garish woman stepped in front of him. "I saw you get off the train. Still got your mustering out pay?"

Neb stepped back and looked at the woman. The men at the post always talked about women, but there were certainly no women at the post or on the troop train. On the way back from Texas, the train had stopped over in New Orleans for a day and a night. He had seen the women on the sidewalk around Jackson Square, but had not paid them much attention. He didn't have to think long.

2

He looked at the woman. He then looked out across the gloomy little town. When he looked back at her, his square jaw was firmly set. His eyes had a piercing glare that would frighten most people. Without speaking, he stepped around her and walked away.

That decision would turn out to be one of the many he would make throughout his life that would serve him well. Decisions that would serve him practically. Decisions that would instill life's virtues for generations.

≈

He started walking. The streets around the train station and close to town were crudely paved with tar. He was sure the tar was the latest upgrade for most travelers. But in July, he could feel the heat rising from it. He passed the hardware store and walked three more blocks. The tar stopped and a plank road took over. In another half-mile, just pass the lumber yard, there were no more businesses and the road turned to dirt. When he reached the outskirts of town there were no houses and he was walking alone through the countryside.

The air was hot and dry. The army boots stirred the dirt on the road and caused small dust clouds around his feet. He removed the woolen shirt and tied it to his belt. He was glad he had filled his canteen. The water wouldn't stay cool, but it would be wet. The dusty road and the heat didn't bother Neb. He suddenly felt good; better than he had in a long time. Physically, his fatigue seemed diminished. Mentally, his spirits were heightened. He didn't know why. He still didn't know what lay ahead for him. Was the unknown giving him this feeling of exhilaration? Was getting close to home making him feel better? Was there still a home? *Maybe,* he thought, *it just feels good to be off that train and out of Gaston.*

Heading toward the place where he was born in 1895, he began to recall his childhood. Now at twenty years old, reflecting on life was something he had never done. He had never particularly thought about life at all. Most of his thought processes, time and energies had been devoted to a kind of day-to-day survival. He did remember that his parents had always seemed old and both had died when he was six. He certainly had experienced some kind of emotional grief then. But it did not last long. One of his sisters, the oldest in the family, had raised him; something she probably would have done anyhow. The older children in most families were expected to help care for the younger children.

Now, walking on the dirt road alone, he was emotionally charged and ready for all life had to offer. He couldn't remember the last time he had felt this good.

His thoughts were interrupted when he heard the sound of horses and a wagon approaching from behind. He stepped to the side of the narrow road to allow them to pass. The farmer, driving the open-bed wagon, stopped along side and without any other greeting said, "That uniform looks pretty hot. You goin' far? I can give you a ride as far as ten miles up the road to Belltown."

Without hesitation, Neb reached up, shook the farmer's hand, "Yes sir. I'd appreciate that very much." He climbed upon the wagon and sat beside the farmer.

After a few moments of silence the farmer spoke first, "There's part of a bushel of scuppernongs back there and some scrawny little apples I wasn't able to sell in town. Help yourself."

Neb took him up on the offer. He was not only hungry; he hadn't had fresh fruit in years.

"Where you goin', son?" the farmer asked.

"McLean."

"You got family there?"

"I'm not sure", Neb replied. "I grew up there before I joined the army. Mama and Daddy died when I was little. There were six of us children. The three girls were the oldest, then us three boys. I was the baby in the family. When my oldest sister, she practically raised me, married a circuit preacher and moved away, I decided to join up. Well, I guess he was a preacher. He sure did drink a lot. Anyhow, I got word while I was in Texas that my other two sisters had gotten married, too. I expect they have moved away by now. I'm not sure where they are."

It felt good to Neb to be talking to someone that had a certain familiarity. Of course, he had talked to the boys at the post and on the train. But, it had always been various kinds of man talk and usually trivial stuff. "I've been in Texas for two years. It feels good to see this kind of country again."

"What become of your two brothers?" The farmer inquired.

"I'm not sure. I haven't had any word from home in six months. The home place was small, just a few acres. I'm assuming my two brothers are still there, and we can keep farming it."

"Son, I don't know what you heard in Texas, but around here the farmers is having a hard time. Especially, us small ones. The big ones are doing okay, but there ain't many small ones left. A lot of the farmers have took to working in the cotton mills. Whole families are working in them mills."

The farmer stopped talking. He could tell from the curious look on Neb's face that he did not fully comprehend what he had said.

The farmer continued, "Yeah, they ain't real big, mostly just little mills, springing up all around here. There's a lot of 'em in and around Gaston. Hell, there's even one in Belltown, no bigger than it is. I'm afraid I'm going to have to take a job in it. But it don't pay enough for me to take care of my family. I'm trying to hold out. But, probably me, my wife and my oldest daughter - she's twelve - will have to go to work in it. They'll hire the kids, you know. In another year my son will be old enough, he can go to work, too. I hate it. But, maybe then we can get by".

Neb knew that a sprinkling of very small cotton mills had popped up in that part of the state before he went to Texas. He had no idea that now there were so many. He continued asking the farmer questions about the mills. To Neb, working in a cotton mill and the life it afforded sounded like a very dismal existence. He was glad he and his oldest brother, John and his second oldest brother, Bascom had the small piece of land. He thought if they worked hard they could make a go of it.

They reached Belltown and the farmer said, "Son, you look tired and you ain't gonna make McLean by dark. You can sleep on my porch tonight. This time of year my wife'll cook up some vegetables from the garden and make a pan of cornbread. If we're lucky, she may even have an apple pie."

As anxious as Neb was to get home to see his brothers, the offer was just too good to turn down. After all this time, one more day wouldn't matter. *Besides*, he thought, *it will probably be the best night's rest and best food I've had in two years.* "That would be mighty nice. If you're sure your wife won't mind."

"She'd love it. Do you think this country is going to get into that war?"

Neb jumped down from the wagon and started helping the farmer with the horses. "Oh, I don't know. I joined up. I didn't have to. But, I can tell you I'm glad I've done my time."

Neb continued the rest of the afternoon and all through supper to enjoy the feeling of relaxation and comfort that had swept over him since he had left Gaston. He was glad he didn't live there. He thought it had seemed dingier than he remembered – at least the part he had seen today. *Was it the mills? Was it the people? Oh well, it doesn't matter.* He didn't care. He didn't live there.

However, lying on the porch later that night - before sleep took over - the easy, comfortable feelings of the afternoon began to drift away. Anxiety and questions filled his head. He started thinking about his two brothers. Would they be re-united? And, what would that be like? They were adults now. As for their physical appearance, the three boys looked a lot alike. They were all tall, with the same Germanic features as Neb. But, appearance was the only characteristic or trait they shared.

John was hard-working, smart and a fast learner. Those qualities, combined with the fact that he was shrewd, would probably serve him well. He had always wanted to get ahead and he was willing to work to get what he wanted.

Bascom, on the other hand, was totally void of any sense of direction, except that of chasing after women, drinking and an all around life of debauchery. No one thought much about it when he would disappear, only to show up two or three days later with black eyes and bruises. Everyone knew he would walk to the local dive, hang out with the ladies, drink and get into brawls. But, when he did come home and set his mind to it, he was a good worker, willing and strapping. And like Neb and John, Bascom knew a lot about farming.

The next morning, rested and eager to see his brothers, Neb thanked the farmer profusely for all his kindnesses and started walking to McLean.

Around 4 o'clock that afternoon, after hitching three rides on various farm and family wagons, he reached the edge of McLean with only about a half-mile left to walk to his old home-place. Neb didn't know it yet, but he had also reached an edge of his life that would effect drastic changes.

3

As he walked across the village he looked around, thinking he might see a familiar face. The houses and roads looked like they hadn't changed at all while he had been away. He didn't see any of the farmers he used to know. Usually some of them were on the roads going to and from their fields. He saw a few children playing in the yards, but not another soul. At this time of the afternoon in July folks were always visible. He decided he couldn't worry about that right now. He was almost home.

His pace accelerated. Shortly, he was walking down a narrow dirt road and soon standing in front of his old, wood frame home on the left side of the road. The closest neighbor, Clyde, lived about fifty feet farther down the road on the right side. There was no activity at Clyde's. The house looked like it had the last time Neb saw it.

Neb stood in front of his house, staring. The doors and windows were all open. There was no sign of life, except for a mule and wagon in the back yard where a small vegetable garden had once been. There was not a garden anywhere now. The yard was overgrown with weeds. The house was never anything more than a small, deficient dwelling. Now, it looked more dilapidated and run down than ever. The paint was almost gone. Some of the clapboards had fallen off. It looked as if no one lived there. *Is the house empty? Where is everybody?* Neb began to feel uneasy.

Hearing footsteps on the dirt, he turned and saw Clyde coming down the road. Neb began to smile, "Clyde, how are you doing?"

Clyde grinned, "Neb, Neb, Neb. For a minute there, I didn't know who you was."

"How are you doing?"

He drawled, "Fine, fine, fine. You just get back?"

"Yes, I just got to town. Where are John and Bascom?"

"Oh, John run down to the general store. He said he'd be back directly"

Still filled with disbelief from the sight of the house, Neb said, "The house sure looks bad."

"Yeah, yeah, yeah," Clyde agreed, slowly nodding his head up and down and finally looking down at the ground.

His neighbor's actions and words, or lack of words, were disturbing. Clyde had always been a big talker, but not today. Everything Neb had witnessed since he got to the edge of town was disturbing. He didn't know why, but he didn't like what he was seeing.

"And where is Bascom?" Neb asked. "Clyde, what's going on?"

Clyde shifted his feet and didn't say anything.

"Well," Clyde slowly started to talk. Appearing to be at a loss for words, he turned and looked down the road as if searching for something. Then his face relaxed and he said, "Oh, here comes John. I'd better mosey along." He spun around and started walking back toward his house.

Neb turned and saw John walking toward him. Now concerned, he walked down the road to meet John. The two brothers embraced with more than the usual affectionate back patting.

John immediately recognized the look of apprehension on Neb's face. Before Neb could say anything, "Let's get you inside out of this sun and out of that uniform. It's hotter than hell out here. I've got some old clothes you can put on. They'll be cooler than that damn thing you're wearing." Not realizing Neb only had one uniform, "Why the hell anybody would put wool in summer uniforms is beyond me."

John had had a propensity for cursing and profanity since the age of ten. Neb would soon learn that John had honed these particular language skills to a whole new level of proficiency in the two years they had been apart. The cursing didn't make him any less accommodating or benevolent. It was simply a habit he made no effort to break.

They walked across the small front yard. One of the steps that led up to the front porch was missing. The two men double-stepped up to the porch. The boards on the porch creaked and gave in so much that Neb was afraid they might break through. He didn't say anything and John made no explanations or excuses. They went inside the little house. It seemed even smaller now than ever before. Neb could not now believe that six children had been raised there. It was a sad sight. Any half-adequate furnishings that had ever been there were gone. The windows were bare. There was a wooden rocker, too dilapidated to sit in and some old wooden crates. He walked through to the room that had served as the kitchen. Even though the house never had running water, it was the room where his Mama first and then his oldest sister had cooked on a wood burning cook stove. The stove was gone. The table and chairs were gone. The room was empty.

Neb tried not to look in John's direction. He didn't want John to see his disappointment. *Is this all that's left of everything I ever knew – my home, my family? What has happened?*

John walked over, touched Neb on the shoulder and said, "Come on, let's go sit on the back porch. It's shady out there. I'll get some fresh water from the well."

Without asking any questions, Neb walked out the back door, glanced around at the overgrown backyard and sat down on the porch steps. He, silent and anxious, waited. He said nothing as John came back across the yard, carrying a bucket of water and a dipper.

John set the bucket on the step between them and started talking. "First, I guess I should tell you about Bascom. The son-of-a-bitch had gone to Gaston to pick up some seed and a few other things. There was a girl there, named Ellie, passing through town on the train. She was on her way from Virginia to Mississippi. She was taking a short lay-over and they got all involved. Well, the bastard ended up going home to Mississippi with her. She told him her father had a huge farm there with growing fields and livestock and he could get some work. I didn't know whether to believe that or not. That was six months ago."

Neb waited.

"Well, when I didn't hear anything, I didn't know what to think. Mississippi is a long way off. I didn't know what the son-of-a-bitch had gotten himself into. I finally got a letter from him last week. Ellie hadn't told him she had been to some fancy school in Virginia. Her father is some kind of animal doctor and really does have a big farm in Mississippi. Bac seems to be doing well. He's working hard and has been a real help with the farm and crops. He also helps the doc take care of the livestock and large animals. He and Ellie are probably going to get married. Her father really likes him. I'm not sure, but I don't think he's drinking quite like he used to. I'm really glad about all that. I think Ellie is going to be good for him."

John continued, "'Course he really put me in a bind here. This piece of land was not turning much profit anyway. I had to take a job at the mill old Mr. McLean built. The hours were long. I couldn't work at the mill and work the land, too. But I did manage to save a little money. I've got it tucked away."

John, weighing every word, continued, "I've had to let the land and house go for taxes. It wasn't making much. It's really been a burden for well over a year now. After tomorrow, it's no longer ours."

Neb felt panic sweep through his entire being. His voice was almost quivering when he spoke, "John."

But before Neb could continue, John said, "Try not to worry. I've figured out a way to pick up a little dairy farm I've seen on the outskirts of Gaston. A woman whose husband died has it for sale. It's too much for her to handle. It's doing okay, but it can do better. She's agreed to sell it to me for a pretty good price. I've got enough saved from working at the mill to make the small down payment. I'm going there tomorrow and close the deal." Then, in a fatherly tone added, "You can come with me."

Neb, trying to relax, "But, what am I going to do then?"

"You can live with me as long as you want. I can't pay you a wage from the dairy. It's not going to pay off for awhile. But you can probably get a job in one of the mills around there. There's a big one there called Firethorn. I heard about a month ago they were hiring."

The panic Neb had felt only moments earlier was gone, replaced with disheartenment. He did not want to go to Gaston, and he certainly did not want to work in a mill. He had never particularly cared for Gaston. After being around the train station and talking to the farmer yesterday, he now liked it even less.

But now, he was desperate. He felt totally helpless and alone in the world. He knew John was trying to help, but it did little to lessen his sorrow. He turned to John and said, "I'll go with you tomorrow. I appreciate what you're doing for me."

≈

The next morning, John hitched the mule to the wagon. He packed his few personal belongings, the rations he had gotten the day before from the general store and some water. The two men loaded everything into the wagon and climbed in. They sat looking at the little home place where they had grown up. They remembered the six children growing up there, some of them barely old enough to remember their Mama and Daddy. There had been some sad times and some happy times. Most of all, there had been hard times. *Today,* Neb thought, *John is probably glad to be leaving.* Neb was not sure what he was feeling. Clyde, who had been watching from his front porch, threw his hand up in a goodbye wave. The two brothers waved back, pulled away in the wagon and started down the dirt street.

≈

The trip was uneventful. The weather was cooler than it had been the day before when Neb had made the same trip in the opposite direction. He was glad for the shirt and pants John had given him. He was certainly cooler and more comfortable in them than he had been in that uniform. However, he did keep the uniform. He knew he could remove the insignia and patches and wear it the next winter if the need should arise.

They enjoyed chatting along the way. John told Neb all the news from in and around McLean. Neb told John all about the army and the long train ride from Texas. He also told John about the day and night stop-over in New Orleans and what he saw of the city. He further explained that he had looked up their daddy's brother, Uncle Elam, and that they had enjoyed a nice visit.

"Oh, I vaguely remember him," John said. "Wasn't he some kind of merchant in that city?"

"Well, he actually has a little bakery just off Canal Street. His wife died a few years ago. But he's doing okay."

The two brothers liked riding along together. The unreserved conversation helped pass the time. The trip seemed shorter to Neb today than it had the day before. They reached the dairy farm, about five miles out from Gaston, that afternoon. The widow, selling the dairy, fed them supper and allowed them to sleep in the barn that night.

The next morning, Neb, John and the widow went into town to the courthouse. The transfer of the dairy, the land and its properties took about an hour.

Afterwards, standing on the courthouse steps John said, "Well Neb, do you want to go by Firethorn Mill and see if you can get a job?"

Neb, inwardly feeling reluctant, outwardly agreed, "That'll be fine."

≈

Neb had not seen many mills and had no idea there were any as big as Firethorn. It was a multi-storied, brick structure. The office where all the business took place was in a smaller, white, wood frame building that stood out in front of the mill. There the hiring was done, the payroll was prepared, cotton was ordered, product was sold and any other necessary business transactions took place.

John sat in the wagon and waited while Neb went inside the office building.

When Neb came walking back out to the wagon, John could see the disappointment on his face. "What's the matter?"

"They were hiring for the weave room and card room three or four weeks ago. But there are no openings now. They did offer me a job as a sweeper. It's the lowest paying job in the mill. I took it."

Neb continued, "There's a housing facility for men, like a dormitory, just down the street from the mill. Since I don't have any way to get from the farm to town each day, I told them I would like to stay there. The rent is not very much. But my paycheck will be so small, that's probably all I can afford."

Neb then turned to John and said, "When I get a day off, or any chance I have, I want to help you at the dairy. I don't expect you to pay me. You've always helped take care of me and I'm very grateful."

≈

The next day Neb moved into the men's dormitory near the mill.

All the property around the mill, for about five square miles, was owned by Firethorn Mill. The area was made up of small city blocks on dirt streets, lined with frame houses also owned by the mill. Workers living in the houses were close enough to walk to their jobs.

The dormitory building was located about a block from the mill. In the block between the back of the dorm and the mill, Firethorn had built a park with a large grassy area where adults could relax and an area with playground equipment for children. It was not uncommon for a mill to provide recreational activities for the workers and their families. The big grassy area had huge trees that provided more than adequate shade for the park benches that had been placed there. In July, when the days were long, workers enjoyed sitting there late in the evenings after having worked in the mill a twelve hour work-day.

The red brick dormitory had three floors with 16 small rooms on each floor. The tiny rooms had only a small bed and dresser. Each floor had a large bathroom at each end of the hall. There was a cafeteria on the ground level, at the front of the building that faced the street.

Neb was comfortable with his living quarters and enjoyed passing time in the evenings in the park. But, he hated his job.

Meanwhile, John waited for Neb to come by the dairy farm. A week passed and John did not hear from Neb. Then two weeks passed. At the end of the third week, Neb's absence began to worry John.

4

The next morning, after Neb had moved into the men's building, he walked to the mill for his first work day. The sun had just come up. It was already hot. It reminded him of reporting to duty in the army in Texas two years earlier, although it didn't seem nearly as important. He reminded himself that it was important; he needed the money. That was the only reason he was going there.

The mill was noisy. From outside on the street, he had heard the never-ending drone emanating from inside the mill. When he went inside, the noise was almost deafening. He wanted to leave. He knew he couldn't. He had no other choice. He climbed five flights of stairs to his assigned area.

Inside, the mill was extremely hot and humid. The air was thick with cotton dust. The dust and lint were so abundant, they had settled on the frames of the huge machines and any other place in the room that was not constantly cleaned. The thick webs of lint hanging from the machines and ceiling looked like ghosts looming over the big room.

He wondered what he should do first and looked around for his supervisor. A worker, with rounded shoulders and arthritic hands, walked up to him, patted him on the back and said, "You'll get use to it." Feeling like a stranger in an even stranger environment, this simple gesture seemed like a welcomed greeting to Neb.

The supervisor showed up next. He told Neb to sweep the floors in the weave room. He instructed him to move throughout the floor in a certain pattern. Neb did exactly as he was told. He pushed the broom up one aisle and down the next between each row of machines. He stopped at the end of each huge machine, gathered the lint and dust from the floor and dumped it in the twenty gallon trash can he pulled behind.

After twelve hours, with only a short lunch break, the whistle blew at 7 o'clock that evening. He went down the stairs and eagerly made his way out of the mill into the fresh air. His clothes were covered with cotton dust. His hair looked almost white where lint had settled on it. The clean, cool air was a relief and it felt good to take a long, deep breath. The clanging of the machines was gone. He welcomed the quiet outdoors.

Except for an occasional hello, he hadn't spoken to many people that day. Walking back to his room, he remembered what the worker with the rounded shoulders had said early that morning. Neb immediately thought to himself, *will I ever get use to it?*

He could not believe what he had seen in the mill that day. Many of the workers looked like children and probably were. He had heard that in some of the mills children as young as ten were working. It was a common practice for women to work in the weave room. Over half the people working in the area where he had swept were women and girls. Neb was accustomed to seeing women and children working on the farms. But he had never seen them working away from their homes or under such appalling conditions.

On his second day at work, he noted several familiar faces and nodded to them. However today, there were three girls he had not noticed before. They huddled together, talking and giggling and looking in his direction. They appeared to be about fifteen or sixteen.

Two of the girls had an undistinguished appearance. The third one, who was not quite so giggly, instantly caught his attention. His focus went to her immediately. She had a presence that evoked an emotion within him he had never experienced before. For fear of seeming awkward, he turned away and continued sweeping.

He thought about the girl the rest of the work-day and as he sat in the park under the shade trees that evening. *Who is she?* He wondered how old she was and why was she working in the mill. She didn't look like any of the other girls working there. She had a slightly polished look unlike the other girls and unlike anyone Neb had ever seen.

The next day Neb saw her again with the same two, giggly girlfriends. He desperately wanted to go over and speak to her. But, he continued sweeping in the direction as instructed by his supervisor.

≈

That evening, sitting under the shade trees, he decided that he was going to go over and speak to her the next day. He didn't know if there would be harmful consequences. He just didn't care. He had to talk to her.

Even though he didn't know exactly what he was going to say, he was excited as he approached her work area the following day. When he went around the end of a loom, his heart sank. The two giggly girls were there, but she was not. He stood at the end of the machine, his shoulders drooped, inwardly cursing himself for not speaking to her before now.

At that moment, he felt a bold tap on his shoulder. *Damn,* he thought, *it's my supervisor.*

He turned and there she was. She was only five feet, four inches tall and she had to look up to speak to him. "Hey there, my name is Nona." She then paused, obviously waiting for him to speak to her.

He looked down at her. He thought her streaked blond hair, blue eyes and smile were the prettiest he had ever seen. He felt sure he was smiling.

He struggled for words. Nothing came. He wanted to say something polite, something pleasant. Finally, "I'm Neb." Then, gaining his composure, "Would you like to come to the park this evening? Would that be alright?" He held his breath, waiting for her answer.

"I'll have to let my mother and sister know where I'm going after work. But then I should be along shortly."

Wow, he thought, *that wasn't so hard.* He began to relax. *I'll wait at a bench under one of the trees.* He watched as she turned and went back to her loom.

≈

Neb went straight to his room after work. He brushed the lint from his hair and hurried down the hall for a bath. Back in his room, he picked through his few clothes and found something clean to wear. After a quick glance in the mirror, he left the room and went to the park to wait.

When he saw Nona approaching, he thought she was the most beautiful sight he had ever seen. She wore a pale pink, cotton batiste dress. The dress had a low-scooped, V-neckline. An artificial flower, also of batiste was pinned at the V. She had brushed her hair out and then swirled it back up around her head. On the side of her hair, there was another artificial flower matching her pale pink dress.

He stood and waited until she reached the bench. "Have a seat. You look very pretty. Is that a new dress?"

"Yes, it's my Sunday dress. My girlfriends, Emma and Ollie, talked me into getting it. You've seen them in the mill."

"How long have the three of you worked there?"

"Oh, not long, only about a month. I won't be able to go back to school in the fall since I got this job. I'm trying to help my Mother and sister."

Neb and Nona sat on the park bench and talked until nearly dark. Each of them wanted to get to know the other one better. Once, when their elbows accidentally touched, he reached for her hand and held it briefly.

"Can you come back tomorrow night?" he asked.

"I'd love to. But I don't think we should talk a lot in the mill."

"Oh, I agree."

"I have to go home now. I don't want my Mother and sister to worry."

Nona left before it got any darker and walked home.

Neb got up and went to the dormitory. He was happier than he had been in a long time as he thought, *tomorrow night I'm going to walk her home.*

≈

The next night they sat on the park bench until dark, their shoulders pressed closely against each other.

When Nona realized how dark it had gotten, she said, "I should go. I don't want to walk home alone when it gets really dark."

Neb, speaking up as if he had truly come to her aid, said, "Oh, I would never let you walk home alone in the dark. I'll walk with you." Inside, Nona was glowing.

As they left the park, they stopped behind one of the big trees. The embrace and kiss that followed was unlike anything they had ever experienced – a sensation reserved for those newly in love.

They continued meeting in the park. Each of them cherished and nurtured their relationship as each night they held hands and kissed behind the tree.

They had been doing this for about three weeks when one night they talked longer and later than usual. As they talked, Neb wiped the tears that fell down Nona's face.

≈

The following morning, Neb did not go to work in the mill. Instead, he went to the same office where he had been hired. He quit his job and picked up the wages he was due.

He then went to the dairy farm. He had something he had to discuss with John and he was truly dreading it.

≈

When Neb reached the farm, he thought it looked better than it had three weeks earlier. The yards were cleaner. Some wood had been replaced on the house and part of it had been painted. The areas around the barns were neat and well kempt. He looked around and didn't see anyone. He went out to the barn where the cows were milked. He found John there washing the big, metal milk cans.

"Morning."

John looked up, saw Neb and without losing the chewed cigar that was stuck in the corner of his mouth, growled, "Where the hell have you been?"

"Working."

"Three weeks is a long time. I was beginning to worry." John set the milk can aside, wiped his hands on his overalls, "Ah, I'm glad to see you. Let's go in the house. I've got someone I want you to meet." As the two men walked toward the house, John reached over and patted Neb on the shoulder. "How've you been doing?" Before Neb could answer, they reached the kitchen door. "Come on in."

The inside of the house was immaculate. The kitchen was sparkly clean and filled with the aroma of a home cooked meal. A pretty young lady was standing in front of the cook stove watching over several steaming pots. Her features were delicate and her eyes sparkled. She looked across the room and smiled at Neb. He was surprised to see a girl there, but he was more surprised by what John said next.

"Neb, this is Virginia. She's another reason I moved to Gaston. We're going to be married next week and we hope you can come to the wedding."

After the proper greetings and congratulations, Neb began to relax a little. It looked like his news might be more palatable for John than he had first thought.

But, before Neb could say anything, John said, "Let's eat."

They sat down at the table. Neb felt he now had the courage and kindly announced, "John, I can't come to your wedding next week. I won't be here. I quit my job this morning and I'm getting married tomorrow."

John looked at Neb, his face void of any expression. He placed his fork on the table and dropped his hands in his lap. "You what? Have you gone crazy? Jobs are hard to find."

Neb went on talking, "I can't work in that mill another day. I've met a wonderful girl I want to marry. And, I certainly won't have her working there. As soon as we're married tomorrow, we're leaving town."

John snarled, "That all sounds well and good. But how do her folks feel about that, how are you going to support her and where the hell do you think you're going?"

"We're going to New Orleans. When I saw Uncle Elam there three weeks ago, he said, 'Neb, why don't you stay here and help me out.' I don't know if he really meant it, but I'm going to find out. You know he and his wife, Aunt Sadie, never had any children. I don't know for sure, but I think he wants to get into the ice cream business."

John sat quietly, listening.

Neb continued, "At the time, I didn't give much thought to what he had said. I had been gone for two years and felt I needed to get back home. But now that I'm here, I don't think there's a lot here for me. My girl, Nona, is sad to leave her family. But she has agreed to come with me."

John, looking bewildered, said, "What will you do if you get there and he really doesn't have a job for you? What the hell will you do then? Why don't you write to him and find out before you go."

Neb said, "You know I'm willing to take my chances. I feel I must make a life for Nona and myself." Privately, he thought, *and I'd sure rather start our life together somewhere besides here.*

John appeared to soften, "Well, I don't know what to think. I hope you'll be okay. Do you have enough money for the train tickets?"

"Yes, I think so. I have a little money from the first two weeks pay check at the mill and all of this week's pay. Thanks a lot. I should be alright. Besides I know you don't have any to spare."

The two brothers talked until late afternoon. They joked, laughed and savored every remaining moment of their visit.

≈

Neb left the dairy farm that afternoon and hitched a ride back to town. He went to the train station to get the tickets for his and Nona's trip the next day. They were planning to leave immediately after the wedding.

When he stepped up to the ticket window, he was met with sickening news. There was a southbound train the next day at the usual time. But he didn't have enough money for two tickets. He had no idea they would cost so much.

He didn't know what to do. Thoughts were racing through his head. He was so upset he could not think clearly. *What am I going to tell Nona?* He hated to go back to John and ask for help. He really didn't know if John could help him. He knew he had to move out of his room since he had quit his job at the mill. He knew he could live with John for awhile, but he couldn't ask to take Nona there. *Where will I find another job?*

He couldn't continue hanging around the train station, pacing. That would not solve the problem. He walked back to his room and began to gather his few belongings. He looked at the white shirt he had kept clean and ironed for the wedding tomorrow. Would he need it now? He picked up his old, woolen uniform he had kept for winter. He had not planned to take it to New Orleans. He certainly wouldn't need it there. He stood staring at the uniform. Tears began to well in his eyes. He had wanted so much for his plan to work out. Now he had no plan at all.

Standing there, totally disheartened, he suddenly remembered the money from the last two pay periods at the army post. It was buttoned up in the breast pocket of the uniform. His life, in the last three weeks, had been filled with so much emotion and he had been working so hard at the mill, he had forgotten that he had put the money away.

He was so thankful he had not spent it in Gaston on that first day back home. He had ignored the floozy. He had made the right decision. Neb had always believed in doing the honorable, decent thing. It was not from fear or sense of duty. It was more from a deeply seeded consciousness, a feeling of self respect for others.

He was in high spirits and excited about the challenges he knew lay ahead.

With a sigh of relief, he dropped down and sat on the edge of the bed. He counted the money. It was a little more than enough. He would go back to the train station and get the tickets. Maybe there would be enough for a small, gold wedding band for Nona. However, they had discussed rings and agreed not to buy them at this time. He knew she couldn't afford to get one for him. He decided to think about that later. Right now, he must get to the train station.

After buying the tickets, he had a little more than enough money left to buy snacks for Nona and himself on the train. He thought about the agreement they had regarding the rings. On his way back to his room, he stopped at The Bon Ton, a small emporium three blocks from the mill. However, he didn't get a wedding band. Instead, he bought a gold locket that hung from a delicate gold chain. It didn't cost very much and he was sure it was not real gold. He was remembering the pale pink dress she had worn the first night they met in the park. He thought the locket would look so pretty with that dress.

5

NONA

She was born and spent her early years in Queens Mountain, a small town about fifteen miles west of Gaston. Most of Nona Alred's childhood memories were centered on the hand-to-mouth existence of her family, or what little family she had.

There were only her mother and sister that she could claim. She had always been told by her mother that her father had died when she was very young. However, as she approached adolescence and began to move around the little town on her own, she heard rumors and talk that her father was an alcoholic. She also heard that he had just left town, never to be seen again, and left his wife and two daughters on their own. She never broached the subject with her mother. She didn't remember her father and she was not the kind of person to let hearsay, true or not, bother her.

Nona felt it should make no difference to her what had happened to her father. Nor, did she dwell on the other difficulties she encountered in her childhood. She was determined not to allow circumstances, especially those over which she had no control, establish a standard or a cushion by which she would live the rest of her life. She felt she had the strength to surmount disadvantages and saw them only as small hindrances. Mature for her age, her goals were not centered on monetary or material gain, but rather a life of compassion, forbearance and composure.

Her mother had always been a sickly sort. From the time Nona was eleven, she could remember her mother's problems with rheumatoid arthritis. She didn't know very much about the disease. She only knew that her mother had difficulty walking and had begun to lose full use of her hands. She and her sister knew that it was only a matter of time before they would have to care for their mother in every respect.

By the time she was fourteen, the little family of three left Queen's Mountain. They moved to Gaston where her sister, Ruby, had gotten a job at Brown Mill, one of the smaller mills there. They were grateful for the work. It not only provided a humble means of existence, it also allowed them to move into one of the three room houses owned by the mill. The wood frame house had two rooms across the front. The room on the left served as a sitting area. The one on the right was the bedroom with two regular beds. The kitchen was on the back of the house behind the bedroom. The wavering floor was partially covered with a piece of worn linoleum with a faded checkered pattern. A small wood table, covered with blue oil cloth with frayed edges, sat in the middle of the room. The table and linoleum had been left there by the former tenants. If anyone had tried to remove them, they probably would have fallen apart. There was a sink that hung on one sidewall and functioned as a kitchen sink and as a basin for personal use. A wooden ice box, insulated with cork and lined with metal, sat on the opposite wall. The delivery iceman brought a block of ice each morning that kept their meager rations cool and provided ice for cold beverages during the hot summer days. The house had minimal electrical wiring in each room that only allowed for a single light bulb in the center of the ceiling. It was one of the smallest houses in the Brown Mill village, but at least it was a roof over their heads.

Nona wanted, more then anything, to go to school. She loved reading and the interaction with the teachers and other students. She tried to attend school after she moved to Gaston. But it became more and more difficult for the little family to get by on Ruby's wages. By the time she was sixteen, Nona started looking for a job. The small mill where Ruby worked was not hiring. Nona's two close girlfriends, Emma and Ollie, told her Firethorn was hiring for the weave room and they were going to try to get jobs there. The three young girls went to Firethorn and were hired. They were delighted when they learned they would be working close to each other in the same area.

Nona had met the two sisters, Emma and Ollie, when she moved to Gaston two years earlier. They were a little silly, but she loved their company and spending time with them. Nona was a happy person and enjoyed meeting new people and chatting. She was able to talk to her girlfriends about everything. They talked about what they wanted to do when they grew up, boys and all the usual things young girls like to talk about. She shared a closeness with them she did not have with her own sister or anyone else.

The three girls began working in the weave room at Firethorn. Nona didn't like working in the mill and longed to be in school. But she enjoyed spending the days with her girl friends and having someone her own age with whom to talk. She had never had any close friends and relished this new-found treat.

She also liked being able to help her mother and Ruby when she gave them most of her first week's wages. She only kept back a small amount for a pink dress she had seen on sale. Since she only owned two or three skirts and blouses she wore to work, she wanted the dress to wear to church. Besides, Emma and Ollie had goaded her into buying it.

Even though she never particularly joined in, Nona never minded that Emma and Ollie were constantly scrutinizing the young men at work and always giggling about one thing or another. It always lightened her day to be around them.

The three girls had been working in the mill for about a month when Emma ran up to Nona one day. Ollie was following close behind, with her hand over her mouth, giggling.

"Nona, Nona," Emma said, "That man over there is staring at you. And boy, he is good-looking."

Nona quietly turned and looked at the man. He was so tall and handsome. She thought he was the best looking man she had ever seen. She shushed Emma and Ollie. She slowly turned back around and began working at her loom. She then thought to herself, *I'll see him again. At least, I hope so.*

The next day the two girls ran up, giggling once more. "Nona, he's back. Go over and speak to him."

Nona, very softly, said, "I'll give him one more day to speak to me. If he doesn't come over here by my loom tomorrow, I'll go over there."

On the third day, Emma and Ollie promised to watch her loom. Nona saw Neb coming at the regular time. She didn't wait for him to speak to her. She didn't want to take any chances. She went straight over and tapped him on the shoulder and said, "Hey there, my name is Nona."

After a short time, Nona went back to her loom. Emma and Ollie were waiting, eager to find out what had happened. "Well, what did he say? What did you say? Is he going to ask you to go out?"

Nona said, "I'm meeting him in the park tonight. Do you think I should wear my new, pink dress?"

"Oh, yes. That would be perfect. Promise, tomorrow, you'll tell us everything that happens."

The three girls couldn't stop talking the next day. Nona told them everything she had learned about Neb the night before and that she was going to meet him in the park again that night. She also told them it must be their secret while at work. Emma and Ollie kept that secret for as long as Nona worked in the mill.

Nona was drawn to Neb with an intensity and warmth that was a whole new experience for her. She quickly recognized his commendable qualities. She felt they shared the same dreams and hopes.

Nona did everything she could to cultivate the relationship with Neb. She did not want to appear too eager. It was not her nature to be extremely forward. However, she had no problem arranging for him to walk her home. She also planned for him to meet her mother and sister on a Sunday afternoon, when she knew no one would be working.

≈

Nona soon realized the seriousness of the relationship and was not surprised when Neb mentioned marriage. However, she was surprised when he wanted to get married so soon. She needed time. She was not prepared to leave her mother and sister. They counted on her to contribute to the household budget and help with the care of her mother. She asked herself what was more important, her desires or the needs of her family.

Moving far away did not bother her. She found that exciting. Not in her wildest fantasies did she ever think of getting married and moving to a city like New Orleans. She knew it wasn't, but it seemed almost like a foreign city to her. She also knew that it would probably be years before she'd see her mother and sister again – if she ever did see them again.

Now that the time had come for decisions, she felt she had so much to consider.

After agonizing deliberation, restless nights and many tears, she told Neb she would marry him.

Now she must tell her folks.

≈

Nona went home that final night, knowing she must tell her mother and sister of her marriage plans. Her stomach ached as she walked into the little house.

Her mother was sitting on the side of the bed. She looked at her daughter's face. "Why have you been crying?"

Nona was barely able get the words out, "I have quit my job. I'm marrying Neb tomorrow and moving to New Orleans."

After a long pause, her mother quietly said, "I hope you've thought about this. Are you sure this is what you want to do?"

Nona nodded.

"Then I think it's a good idea. He's a fine young man. You deserve a good man in your life, something you've never had."

Ruby sat expressionless, her hands folded in her lap. She finally looked up, glared at Nona, got up and left the room without saying a word.

≈

Nona, not having slept very much during the night, rose the next morning before Ruby left the house for work. She went into the kitchen where Ruby was making coffee. She knew there was nothing she could say or do to redeem herself. She didn't try. She just said, "I'm really going to miss you. I promise to write as soon as we get there."

Ruby, having softened very little, said, "I'm sorry I can't go with you to the courthouse for your wedding today. As you know, I have to go to work." Then, she somewhat acerbically, said, "Somebody has to take care of Mama." Without saying anything more, she hugged Nona around the neck and left for the mill.

Nona stood motionless in the dreary kitchen. All the questions she had asked herself so many times before began, once again, racing through her head. *What should I do? Should I marry Neb or stay here and help support my family? I love Neb so much. I can't think of disappointing him. I won't disappoint him.*

Nona put on her pink dress and packed her few clothes. She went over and sat on the edge of her mother's bed. They talked about the weather and other insignificant subjects. When she realized how much time had passed, she hugged her mother and said, "I have to go now. I'm supposed to meet Neb at the courthouse at nine o'clock sharp."

Her mother returned the hug and a kiss on the cheek, "I'm sorry I'm not able to walk with you to your wedding. Please be careful and write just as soon as you can."

Nona left the little mill house and headed toward downtown. She thought to herself as she walked alone, carrying her small satchel. She hoped her mother and sister would be alright. She wondered if her girlfriends would miss her. She knew she would miss all of them. She also knew that she would love New Orleans and could not wait to be with Neb. She truly believed she had made the right decision.

≈

She reached the courthouse at exactly nine o'clock.

The large, gray stone building had wide steps that led up to the main entrance. As she stood at the bottom of the steps, looking up, she did not see Neb anywhere. She glanced around the sidewalk in front of the building and did not see him. For an instance she felt heartbroken. She thought, *what will I do if he's not here?* The queasiness in her stomach intensified. *Where is he?* That's when she knew she and Neb were meant to be together. She wanted a life with him more than anything.

A certain composure suddenly came over her. The calmness she now felt assured her she was doing the right thing. She quickly climbed the steps and went inside to a large entry hall. She had never been in the courthouse and didn't know where she should go. She stood quietly in the middle of the hall. She heard someone softly call her name. When she looked to her right, she saw a small ante room. Neb was standing in the door to the room. She thought he looked so handsome in his white shirt. *Is he really going to be my husband?*

As she walked up to him, she realized he was holding the marriage license in one hand and a small box in the other.

Neb lightly kissed her cheek and said, "The judge said to wait here. He'll call us for us in a few minutes. In the meantime, I have a gift for you."

He opened the small box, removed the locket and put it around her neck. It was, without a doubt, the finest gift she had ever received and the most important he had ever given.

≈

They got married that morning in the judge's chamber and began their journey to New Orleans. They also began their journey through their life together.

A life together that would be filled with love, happiness and prosperity. But these things would be integrated with heartache and despair that would test their convictions beyond belief. If they had known all they would face on this journey, would they have started out?

6

NEW ORLEANS

The two young people stood on one side of Decatur Street looking across at the bakery. Neb and Nona Kohler were wondering what Uncle Elam's reaction would be when he saw them. They had talked about it on the train and realized that they really didn't have a back-up plan. Standing there now, they were frightened. What if the uncle didn't have a job for Neb or was not able to help them in any way? What would they do then? They didn't know anyone else in New Orleans. They didn't have enough money to get back to Gaston. They were delaying crossing the street and going into the shop. They were afraid the answers might be ones they didn't want to hear.

They were both exhausted. The train trip had been long. It was now two o'clock on an August afternoon in New Orleans and the heat and humidity were oppressive. The streets were wet from the usual afternoon thunderstorm. The steam rose from the pavement and made breathing difficult. With every breath they felt like they were drowning. Beads of sweat trickled down their foreheads and down their necks. They were holding hands even though their hands were wet with sweat.

They had been so elated after the wedding ceremony, and had loved spending time together on the trip south. They had never been alone together for such a long period, even though they weren't really alone on the train. They had cuddled close to each other and held hands almost constantly. Nona had laid her head on Neb's shoulder and slept for over an hour.

From the moment they stepped off the train at the station and started walking to the bakery, Nona had been captivated by the sights of the city. Neb was overjoyed with her enthusiasm. He had told her a little about New Orleans, at least the parts he had seen. She had vowed she was going to love it. He had no idea she would be so zealous on this first day when she was so tired.

But now they must cross the street and go into the bakery. They looked at each other, each inwardly hoping for good news. Dodging the streetcar, they made their way across the wide street. The black-top street was even hotter then the sidewalk and their slippery, sweaty hands lost their grip before they got across. When they were safe on the other side, they stood looking up at the sign on the shop – "Kohler Bakery". Having reached their destination created more doubt and anxiety in their minds. Had they made the right decision?

They stepped into the bakery, not really hearing the little bell that rang over the door. They were overwhelmed with the aroma. The place smelled wonderful. Neither of them had ever smelled or eaten breads or rolls made with yeast. The aroma of the spices sweetened the air. The small, front area where baked goods were sold had a long case, with a glass front, across the middle of the room. The case was filled with an array of fruit pies and sweet rolls. There was a table along each side wall covered with white oil-cloth. Each table was piled high with different kinds of loaves of bread, sitting unwrapped on the oil cloth. Neb had not given the goods in the bakery much attention when he had been there a few weeks earlier. Nona stood in amazement as she looked around the room. They didn't speak. They were both absorbed in what they saw and smelled. It was a new experience. There were only two bakeries in Gaston, and they never had all these varieties of breads and baked goods.

Their focus was interrupted when Uncle Elam came through the door from the back room. A tall, thin gentleman, he wore a long, bib apron covered with grease spots and flour. He pulled a handkerchief from his pocket and mopped his brow. Expecting a customer, he broke into a big smile when he saw Neb. "Well son, isn't this a surprise. I never really expected to see you again and certainly not this soon. I hope you've come back here to help out your ol' uncle."

Neb immediately walked over and gave his uncle a big hug and slap on the back. He then said, "Uncle Elam, I'd like you to meet my wife. This is Nona. We got married yesterday."

Uncle Elam looked at Nona. Trying to disguise his mild embarrassment, he said, "Oh, I see. Is this like a honeymoon or something?"

Neb said, "Well, I guess you can call it a honeymoon of sorts. But, I've really come here looking for a job."

Uncle Elam, very kindly said, "Well, you've come to the right place. This just tickles me to death. I hope you'll help me out here in the shop. We can discuss the arrangements later. Do you have a place to stay?"

"No."

"As you know, my apartment over the bakery is small. However, I have just acquired the vacant space next door. It has a tiny room and bath upstairs. It's not much, but the two of you are welcome to stay there. If you decide to stay on and work with me, it's yours as long as you want it."

Uncle Elam's words were like a blessing from heaven to Neb and Nona's ears. They wanted him to say it again just to make sure they heard correctly. Neb was grinning. "Uncle Elam, I can't thank you enough."

The uncle thought for a moment and asked, "Y'all been on the train all night?"

"Yes," they both said.

"Y'all must be exhausted. You kids go on up to the room and get some rest. Then we'll have supper. After that we'll talk tonight and see what we can work out about a job. I've got some other news I'll tell you about. But first, wait here just a minute."

He left the youngsters and went into the back room.

Neb and Nona just stood still and smiled at each other. They felt a huge burden drift away. Uncle Elam's kindness was more generous than they had dared to dream and beyond all their expectations.

In a few minutes, the uncle came out carrying two tall glasses of lemonade that he gave to the newlyweds. He went to the long case and took out several big, fluffy rolls covered with powdered sugar, then reached in his pocket and took out a key. He handed over the rolls and the key and said, "Here's the key to the room. I'll call you when supper's ready."

Neb smiled and shook his head up and down in a positive gesture. Sixteen year-old Nona was so overwhelmed; she impulsively threw her arms around her new uncle and squeezed his neck in gratitude.

≈

Later that evening, after Uncle Elam had closed the bakery, he called the two for supper.

On the way up to his apartment, they walked back through the bakery and into the back room where all the baking took place. The three walked around the room as Elam showed them all the equipment and explained how it all worked. He showed them the big ovens that had no thermometers or thermostats. He demonstrated how you open the big oven door and wave your hand around inside to check the temperature. There were two ovens kept at different temperatures to bake the varied products. There were huge, colorful, cloth bags of flour and sugar stacked in the back corner. The tables in the other corner held large, brown paper bags filled with salt, leavening agents, cinnamon and other spices.

The uncle let the two look around the room a few minutes. Then he said, "Let's go upstairs. I've got some supper on the stove."

They went up the stairs at the back of the work area to the small apartment where Uncle Elam lived. It was neat and cozy with a sitting room, a kitchen and a small bedroom to the side of the kitchen. He said, "I guess I could have a bigger place, but I'm comfortable here and I like being close to my work. My work has pretty much been my whole life since Sadie died".

The kitchen was tiny. There was just enough room to walk around a small table with chairs, a three burner stove and two small cabinets. The table and cabinet tops were all covered with white oil cloth with a red and yellow flower design. The four chairs around the small table were painted with bright red, enamel paint. The kitchen was neat and clean, except for the pots of food staying warm on the stove.

The older gentleman put the meal on the table and the three sat down to eat.

Nona could not decide which was more delicious, the macaroni and cheese or the spicy beans. She was not accustomed to noodles or any kind of spicy food. The sweet, rich coffee with hot milk was unlike any she had ever had.

When Uncle Elam saw her delight over the food, he said, "Apparently, you're not accustomed to this kind of food?"

She replied, "No, I'm not. I think it's wonderful. I can't wait to learn to cook like this. I'm sure there're many dishes I can learn to fix. I especially love this coffee. I hope we have it again in the morning for breakfast."

Uncle Elam chuckled and said, "Oh, we'll be having it all the time,"

As they ate and chatted, Nona told the uncle a little about her family and that she had been worried about leaving her mother and sister. But she didn't tell him about her father's questionable alcohol addiction and disappearance. She told him about working in the mill and her two girlfriends. She also explained how she and Neb had met.

Uncle Elam asked Neb about John and Bascom and the three sisters. Neb shared all the news he had gleaned during the three weeks he had been in Gaston.

"Come on Neb," Uncle Elam suggested. "Let's go sit in the living room."

Nona made her way around the table and cleared the dishes. She washed them in the sink and began to stack them in the drain on the sideboard.

Uncle Elam went to a small desk and brought back two cigars and handed one to Neb, "Smoke?"

"Sure."

Elam reached in his pocket, got some matches and handed one to Neb. As he sat down in a big over-stuffed chair, pulled up a footstool and propped his feet up, he motioned for Neb to have a seat. Both men leaned back with their heads on the backs of their chairs. It wasn't long after they lit their cigars that the small apartment was flooded with the mellow smell of tobacco. Uncle Elam tilted his head back and looked up at the ceiling. After a moment, he turned in his chair and looked in the direction of the kitchen where Nona was just finishing the dishes. "Come over here and sit down, little lady. I want to talk to you too."

Nona put the dish cloth under the sink and went in to sit with the two men in the cloud of cigar smoke.

The uncle began to explain. "As I mentioned this afternoon, I've just leased that space next door. I want to put a coffee parlor in the room on the street level. Of course, you kids can keep the bedroom and bath upstairs."

He continued, "I want a place where people can sit and have a cup of coffee and maybe a sweet roll. I don't have enough room for anything like that here on the bakery side. There's a lot of profit in selling beverages and we're already making rolls."

What their uncle said next really excited Nona and Neb, "I think I want to sell ice cream, too. You know those waffle cones people have started making? Well, I've found I can make them in the bakery and they're pretty good. There's a little Creole kid been coming around here looking for odd jobs. I could pay him a few cents a day to churn a couple of buckets of ice cream. It can set in the buckets of ice each day 'til it's all sold. People are really fascinated with ice cream cones. Actually, they're going crazy over cones of ice cream. If the parlor business does well, I can cut a door in the wall between the bakery and the parlor. The landlord said it would be alright. Frankly, I think it will increase business in the bakery, too."

He went on, "Nona, I think a pretty, young lady like you could run that place for me. That is, if y'all aren't opposed to women working outside the home."

Nona could hardly sit still. She was so thrilled with Elam's confidence in her and at the prospect of a job.

Elam kept talking, "Neb, I've already got more than I can do in the bakery. I could sell more baked goods if I had some help. And with the addition of the parlor, there'll be even more work. I sure wish you'd consider working here. 'Course, I intend to pay both of you for your jobs. The wages may be a little low at first, but you can have the room at no cost. If business goes like I think it will, we'll increase that pay in no time. New Orleans is growing, especially here in this downtown area. There are more electric streetcars than ever before and people are able to get around easily. I think it's ready for something like this. However, if you need time to think about my offer, I'll understand."

The newlyweds looked at each other, smiling. Neither of them could believe what they were hearing.

Nona looked at her new uncle and then at her husband and said, "I can't think of anything I'd like better. I would love living here and working in the coffee parlor. I can't wait to write to everybody in Gaston and tell them I'm going to sell ice cream. They'll never believe – ice cream - of all things."

Neb was overjoyed. He liked his uncle's offer and was so proud of his new bride. He sat up in his chair, slapped his uncle on the knee and said, "It's a deal." Then with a smile in his voice, he added, "Uncle Elam, you'll never know how grateful we are. We can't thank you enough."

The uncle then offered another suggestion, "Tell you what, you folks walk around the city tomorrow and learn your way around a little bit, especially you Neb. We're going to start making a few bread deliveries and I'll be needing your help with that. There's a convent and school over on Lafayette Street that's going to start placing an order every day and they'll expect delivery on a daily basis. You're going to need to know where things are. So you kids relax and have a nice day tomorrow. I'll order the tables and chairs and other supplies we'll need for the parlor. We can set it all up the next day and get ready for business."

After the two left for their room, Elam sat in his little living room, smoking his cigar and softly mumbling. "It's a real blessing that the youngsters have come into my life right now. I think they're good, hard-working folks and are going to be a real asset in this business. And they're my brother's children. I like having family here. I've been alone too long. I hadn't realized how lonely it has been. It feels good to be needed."

≈

When Neb and Nona got to their room that night, they felt like newlyweds more than ever. Most of all, they felt like newlyweds that had been blessed with a wonderful wedding gift, a wedding gift not only from Uncle Elam, but also from Heaven.

≈

The newlyweds woke the next morning ready for the day and the ventures that lay ahead.

Neb went to the bakery and got some stationery from Uncle Elam. He also brought cups of hot coffee and sweet rolls back up to the room. While they enjoyed their small breakfast, they each wrote short notes to their families. Nona, of course, wrote to Emma and Ollie. They told of their safe arrival and developments thus far. For a brief moment while writing, they thought of John's and Ruby's and Nona's mother's welfare. But their concern was short-lived. They were both so absorbed in their own happiness and good fortune. The mill and the dismal directions of their lives in Gaston were quickly being erased from their memories. They were in love and so appreciative of the opportunities that had been offered them.

When the coffee was finished and the letters were sealed, they left the little room and began walking. The walk from the train station the day before had permitted only a brief preview of the city. They felt good this morning, as they walked up and down the streets of New Orleans. They held hands, brushed each other's shoulder and talked. They were not accustomed to the wide streets and could not believe there were so many electric streetcars. While strolling through Jackson Square, they stood for minutes in awe of St. Louis Cathedral. Nona had never seen a cathedral before and felt like she was in a foreign country. She tried not to stare at the many nuns that were making their way up and down the sidewalks. But she was not shy. She stopped and talked to the street vendors pushing carts and selling everything from fruit and vegetables to fresh fish. She had never seen such sights and interesting people. The smells of the city were so different from Gaston. She could smell fish and coffee and other cooking odors mixed with the hot-oily smell of the streetcars moving on the metal tracks. The vendors, selling their wares, spoke with an accent she had never heard before. She sometimes had trouble understanding what they were saying. Passers-by spoke with yet another accent.

Neb found Lafayette Street where the convent and school were located. They stood outside the wrought-iron fence staring at the establishment. The yard was full of uniformed children laughing and playing while nuns strolled around in pairs chatting. While standing in front of the school, Neb looked down and saw tears in Nona's eyes.

With great concern, he asked, "What's the matter? Is something wrong?"

"Oh no," Nona replied. "I think it would be so nice to go to school there. Of course, I'll never get to go to school again. But, wouldn't it be wonderful if our children could go there someday?"

Hearing her words made Neb even more hopeful that their life there would be happy and prosperous. He was so glad they had decided to come to this city.

They then walked down St. Charles Place and gawked at the large, beautiful houses. They meandered in and out of the French Quarter. They both saw sights that day unlike anything they had ever seen anywhere in their lives. They were totally fascinated and enraptured with the city.

They returned to the bakery late in the afternoon and began telling their uncle of all the people, sights and sounds they had experienced.

Uncle Elam could see their delight and said, "I'm glad you like it. I hope you'll be happy here. Neb, why don't you help me clean and close up the bakery? Nona, you go upstairs and start our supper. You might as well get used to that kitchen. It looks like we'll be sharing it for awhile."

The uncle had sounded almost apologetic when he mentioned the kitchen. But Nona didn't mind. Walking up the stairs to the little apartment, she thought to herself, *It's far better than I'm used to.*

She made sandwiches of cold, processed meat and cheese on hard rolls. When the men came up they brought a pie from the bakery and Elam showed her how to make the coffee she loved so much.

Lying in bed later that night, before they each went to sleep, neither Neb nor Nona said anything out loud. But each was thinking, *I really don't miss anything about Gaston and I hope I never have to go near that mill again.*

≈

Early the next morning the uncle and two youngsters started preparing the coffee parlor for business.

The dark-skinned, Creole boy came by the bakery, as usual, looking for odd jobs. Uncle Elam gave him a paint brush and a can of white paint and showed him how to paint the walls of the parlor.

Neb arranged the red and black, small, metal chairs and tables around the room. He then brought in a glass enclosed case and a small counter and placed them near the back of the room.

Nona polished and shined all the fixtures. She placed paper doilies in the glass case that would display the sweet bakery items and ice cream cones. The counter would be used for taking customer orders and collecting money.

The boy, who had painted the walls, had been tickled to get the little job. Except for making sure that everyone knew his name was Luke, he had worked quietly and efficiently during the day. Uncle

Elam was pleased and asked him to come back the next morning to churn ice cream.

At the end of the day, Elam, Neb, Nona and Luke looked around the parlor. They were too tired to talk about it, but their nods of approval said enough. It looked so inviting; they were extremely pleased with their efforts.

≈

Indeed, the coffee parlor was inviting. When Nona opened the doors the following morning, customers immediately came in, placed orders and sat at the little tables to sip coffee and visit with friends. The glass case soon needed to be replenished with sweet buns. Luke churned two buckets of ice cream that were sold out by two o'clock that afternoon.

Nona was more than pleased at the end of the day. She had not only handled her duties with effectuality, she had really loved the interchange with the customers. Of course, Uncle Elam's pat on the back was extremely rewarding.

Neb and Nona did not get to see very much of each other that day. While Nona had been managing the parlor, Neb had been in the bakery learning all the recipes and cooking procedures. He had not only been captivated by the operations of the bakery, he was proving to be a praise-worthy apprentice.

At the end of the day the newlyweds, holding hands, went up the stairs to their room over the coffee parlor. The old uncle went up the back stairs of the bakery to his apartment. He stopped when he reached his small sitting area. He paused and in his usual habit of talking aloud to himself said, "I'm so thankful the children decided to come here."

7

There were many more good days for the Kohler family. Eventually, the good days would become good months and good years.

The city was flourishing and business in the bakery and coffee parlor was growing. Profits increased and were shared proportionally with the young couple.

Neb and Nona were able to save some money. Nona would occasionally slip a few dollars in the letters she wrote regularly to her mother and sister. She and Neb had decided it was the proper thing to do.

However, after a number of months, they decided that all extra monies should be saved. Sending money back to Gaston would have to be suspended for awhile. Nona was pregnant. They knew that eventually they would need bigger living quarters. They would have to move from their little room over the bakery and start paying rent somewhere.

They, along with Uncle Elam, also knew that Nona could not continue working in the coffee parlor. They would have to find someone to take her place.

Luke, who had always shown up religiously to churn the ice cream, said, in his combination accent, "My mama, her name be Mamie Boudreau. She looking for a job and a place to stay. Daddy left and we havin' a hard time."

So it was decided, Neb and Nona would move out of the little room over the parlor and Mamie and Luke would move in. Mamie would take over Nona's duties and manage the parlor.

The Kohlers, expecting a baby, found a house for rent on Erato Street. Nona, who stayed in close touch with Emma and Ollie, wrote:

"Dear Emma,

Guess what. I'm expecting. I don't know who is more thrilled, Neb or me. We're moving into a nice house on Erato Street. It's a neat, white, six-room house called a shotgun house. It has a long hall down the middle of the house with three rooms on each side of the hall. Folks always say, 'If you stood on the front porch and shot a gun through the front door, the bullet would go straight down the hall and come out the back door.' It's just a short streetcar ride for Neb to get to work each morning. With the money we've saved, we were able to furnish most of the rooms. Things are going well here and Neb and I are so happy. I'll write to Ollie tomorrow. If you have time, please go by and speak to Mama. Give her a hug for me. Let me know if you decide to marry Walter. And, I'll keep you informed on my health and pregnancy. Love, Nona."

≈

Nona's pregnancy was difficult and she began labor at seven and a half months. The baby, a daughter, was born prematurely. Even though Nona was in the city hospital for the birth, her doctor, Dr. Hountha, was not able to save the infant. The young couple was devastated. They knew Nona had far better care than she would ever have received in Gaston where so many babies were born at home with minimal health care. But that knowledge gave them little, if any, solace.

Comfort soon came when Nona realized she was pregnant a second time.

However, sensing discomfort and ill health before three months into the pregnancy, she visited Dr Hountha.

Following his examination, the doctor said, "Nona, I want you to go straight home and go to bed. I'll come by tonight after work and talk to you and Neb."

That night sitting in the bedroom where Nona was positioned in bed, Dr. Hountha had a serious look on his face. Addressing the young couple, he said, "I'm pretty sure Nona is pregnant with twins. I doubt she'll be able to carry them to full term." He was silent for a moment and then continued, "I'm very concerned over Nona's health." He paused and then looked straight at Neb. "This could become a life threatening situation for Nona. But my religious convictions will not allow me to do anything more for her. If you wish to find another doctor, please do so." He turned toward the bed. "In the meantime, Nona, you should stay in bed." He slowly got up and left the room. Neb and Nona looked at each other. What should they do? What kind of decisions would they face? Could Nona die?

Nona stayed home alone, lying in bed, while Neb worked long days at the bakery. The nuns at the convent where Neb delivered bread had become good friends. They allowed him to borrow books from their lending room - books that he took home for Nona. Even though she read them with zeal, her mind was constantly focused on the babies. In spite of what Dr. Hountha had said, she tried not to think of her own health. She had to take care of the two babies she was carrying. She stayed in bed. She read. She waited.

Nona followed the doctor's instructions. She was given the best care. But it was not enough. She delivered the babies - a boy and a girl - far too soon. They did not live. If miscarriage of the twins so early in the pregnancy saved Nona's life, no one knows. There were no life-saving choices or decisions that had to be made. Neb and Nona did not change doctors. In spite of his religious convictions, they trusted Dr. Hountha as a doctor.

After a period of bed rest and care, Nona had fully recuperated. Neb's main concern was his wife's health. He knew he would never sacrifice her health for a baby. But Nona still wanted babies. She would walk by the school, after returning books to the convent, and watch the children playing in the school yard. She remembered her first days in New Orleans when she saw the school. She wished she had children she could someday send to that school. She wished she could just have children.

≈

Nona became pregnant again. She committed herself to bed rest. Dr. Hountha would come by, periodically, in the evenings to visit. But once again she delivered prematurely, this time a son that did not live.

≈

Neb's heart ached for his wife. She had lost four babies. In an effort to cure her grief, he suggested that she might enjoy going to the coffee parlor each day to help Mamie. She agreed. She liked being back at work and chatting with the customers. She and Mamie got along famously and Nona loved having a girlfriend.

Business was good in both the parlor and the bakery. Uncle Elam had cut a large doorway between the two businesses making them seem as one. He had also hired additional help for Neb and Mamie. A young boy had come in to help Neb with deliveries and clean-up. A young girl was there helping Mamie with her chores.

Luke would begin churning ice cream early each morning and churn throughout the day. As each churn was ready, he would pack the buckets that held the ice cream in salted ice. He then covered the buckets with used newspapers as a means of insulation. The ice cream was ready for service and available to customers all day long. And the customers came in droves all through the year. New Orleans weather was always hot or at least warm. Ice cream was all the rage and everyone loved it.

Nona enjoyed being back at the parlor. But it was not too many months before she was pregnant again. She immediately stopped going to work each day and, once again, committed herself to bed rest. She was determined to carry this baby to full-term.

Dr. Hountha felt that the progress and developments were much more promising with this pregnancy. Neb and Nona were encouraged and hopeful. But two weeks before the baby was due, Nona went into labor. The expectant parents were frightened as they made their way to the hospital and Dr. Hountha was called in. But their fear was short-lived when she delivered a fine, healthy baby boy. The baby was named Nevette after his father. It was decided that Neb would continue to be called by his nickname of Neb and the new son by the full name of Nevette. Nona was ecstatic. She finally had a baby.

Neb and Uncle Elam decided to hire more help for the coffee parlor. They agreed that Mamie should spend a portion of her work day at the house on Erato Street; certainly until Nona got back on her feet. Besides, Luke had, in a few years, become quite the grown boy. With the additional help he was capable of managing the coffee parlor and taking care of the demands for ice cream.

It was a good arrangement for everyone. There were multiple benefits for all involved. Luke and Mamie had a place to live and a fair income. Neb and Nona had a home, a son and a good job that paid well. Uncle Elam had family close by and a growing business - a business that was booming.

Mamie loved spending part-days with Nona at the house and continued going there daily long after Nona had recovered from the childbirth. She helped with all the household chores and the laundry. She especially liked taking care of Nevette and spoiled him far more than his parents. Nona had help and Mamie had a job she loved. But more importantly, Mamie and Nona got along admirably. They each found that they not only had a girlfriend, but a true friend.

Their friendship would grow. Mamie would become part of the family. She would remain with the Kohlers for as along as she lived, taking care of her duties and spoiling more and more children.

8

THE '20s

The 1920's, after The Great War, were good years for a lot of people in America. There were pockets of prosperity all across the nation. Economic and social changes were abundant. Automobiles had gotten cheaper and more and more people were able to own cars. Families were moving to the cities and women were beginning to venture out of the home in search of employment. It was a time of great invention, especially in the field of electrical innovation, thus giving rise to cheap refrigeration. A greater portion of the population was enjoying more luxuries than ever before. The '20s were good years for many. This certainly included the Kohlers.

Late one evening, after the bakery and coffee parlor had closed; Uncle Elam approached Neb. "Let's go upstairs. There's something I need to discuss with you."

When they got to the little apartment, both men lit their ceremonial cigars and sat at the little kitchen table. After the smoke had filled the small room, Uncle Elam said, "I guess you've noticed that empty shop that has become available next to the coffee parlor? I'm considering taking it on"

"Why?" Neb asked. "We already have two store spaces"

"I want to expand the ice cream business. I think it is going to get even bigger. I want to get one of those refrigerated chests and start selling ice cream by the carton. Folks can not only have a cone of ice cream; they'll also be able to carry a carton home. Most families in New Orleans now have electric refrigerators in their homes. Sure, we'll have to hire more help, but I'm confident it'll be a thriving business."

Elam went on, "We'll keep the bakery and we'll still sell coffee in the coffee parlor. They're both making good money. But we'll also expand the ice cream business, many times over. 'Course, you'll be getting another raise."

Neb agreed it was a good idea and he was tickled over the prospect of still another raise. He could not wait to get home to tell Nona the news. He was sure the streetcar went a little slower than usual that evening. It finally reached his street and he got off.

Nona was always sitting on the front porch waiting for him or in the kitchen finishing dinner. When he entered the house, she was propped up in the bed reading. She put her book down, "You're so late."

"Yes", Neb said, "I stayed late to talk to Uncle Elam. But, I've got good news."

With a big smile on his face and in his voice, he told Nona everything that had transpired during his meeting with Uncle Elam.

Nona listened intently, also smiling.

When Neb had finished talking Nona said, "I'm very pleased over your news, but I also have good news. I'm pregnant again. Isn't that wonderful? Nevette will have a little brother or sister. Hopefully, a little sister." Both were pleased with this news and not really surprised.

≈

The months passed smoothly. With Dr. Hountha's supervision and Mamie's loving attention, Nona gave birth to another son. Once again, the birth of the baby was premature.

Dr. Hountha left the delivery room after the birth and found Neb sitting in the waiting room. He put his arm around Neb's shoulder. "Neb, the baby is alive right now. But he's mighty small. I can't promise you that he'll make it. I have him in an incubator."

"A what?" Neb asked.

"An incubator. It's one of the latest inventions. It's a cabinet where the air and humidity are controlled and hopefully kept just right for the baby until he grows a little more."

Neb, remembering Dr. Hountha's comments from an earlier time, interrupted the doctor. "Is Nona alright?"

"Oh, yes. She's fine. I'm just worried about that baby. Nona can go home in a few days. But I think the baby should stay here in the incubator where we can watch him. We'll go ahead and fill out the birth certificate. Have you folks chosen a name?"

"We sure have. His name is going to be Elam."

Dr. Hountha started to leave the waiting room when a nurse rushed in. "Doctor, I think the Kohler baby is having an epileptic seizure. You need to come right away."

Neb slowly sat down on the sofa and waited.

When the doctor finally returned, he sat down beside the waiting father. "Neb, the baby did not have an epileptic seizure. That rarely happens in babies this age. But this is not a healthy baby. If he makes it, I doubt he'll have a very long life. If I can get him through this, he may make it 'til adolescence."

"Will you come with me to tell Nona?" Neb asked.

≈

When Neb and the doctor entered Nona's room, she looked at their faces. She immediately asked, "What's wrong? Is the baby alive?"

The doctor told her the same things he had explained to Neb.

Nona calmly said, "This baby, our little Elam, is going to make it. You just let us know when we can take him home."

Two weeks later, the Kohlers took their new baby home.

≈

Uncle Elam more than achieved the goals of his business plan. Sales of ice cream were even greater than he had anticipated. Profits from the combination of the three establishments were substantial.

By the second half of the decade, the Kohlers had two more boys, named Ray and Joe. Joe's full name was Joseph Hountha; so named after the doctor that had cared for Nona through the years.

Neb and Nona were conscientious parents and mild disciplinarians, leaving all the spoiling up to Mamie. They were proud of the well mannered, well behaved children.

Mamie had begun spending full days at the house. Because of Mamie's capable help, Nona was able to spend a lot of time with the boys. She took them to the park when she was not pregnant. When she was pregnant, she read books to them - books she had borrowed from the nuns at the convent. She started teaching each child to read well before he came of school age.

Nona was glad when Neb came home from work and announced, "You know, Sister Mary, at the convent, thinks Nevette will be going to school there. Since we're not Catholic, I didn't say one way or the other."

Nona said, "That would be wonderful. Will they let him do that?"

"Yes, but I don't know what your family and friends in Gaston will think and say. They've never been around very many Catholics and might not understand."

Nona retorted, "I don't care what they say, I have never cared what people may say. He's a smart little boy. I want all the boys to have the best education they can get."

Neb just smiled and nodded and said, "That's fine. I'll make the arrangements with Sister Mary."

Nona smiled and said, "Why don't we just find out what they will say." She then laughingly and lovingly said to Neb, "I have wanted to visit Mama and Ruby. I haven't seen them in years. And Mama wants to see the boys. If I'm going to Gaston at any time, I had better go now while I'm not pregnant." She paused for a moment. "All kidding aside, Nevette will be starting school soon. I think now is the time to go."

Neb responded, "I think now is a perfect time. With the new project coming up at work I'll be very busy for a couple of weeks. But do you think you can manage all four children on the train? The baby is still so young."

"Of course I can. They're well-behaved little boys. And the porters will help me. It'll be a wonderful trip."

≈

Arrangements got underway for the trip. Nona wrote a letter to her mother letting her know she was coming. She also wrote to Emma and Ollie with whom she had ardently corresponded through the years. "I can hardly wait to see you and meet your husband and little children. Since the three of us have always been like sisters, I think our children should call us Aunt Nona, Aunt Emma and Aunt Ollie."

Neb wrote to John and asked him to meet Nona and the children at the train station in his new car.

Nona bought gifts for everyone in Gaston. They were gift wrapped, then specially wrapped again so they could be checked through on the train.

Neb went to the train station and bought all the tickets.

Mamie ironed and prepared all the clothes for the trip. Her face beamed when Nona gave her money and asked her to go shopping. She was to choose a few new suits for Nevette and the two toddlers and two new dresses for the infant.

Mamie came back from her shopping trip with a big grin on her face. She showed Nona all the purchases. They had been selected at one of the best shops in New Orleans. Nona thought they were perfect and thanked Mamie for a job well-done.

However, there was one package still laying on the table and Mamie was still grinning. Nona could see the pleasure in Mamie's face.

Nona looked at the package and then looked at Mamie, "What's that?"

"Miss Nona, I went by the convent and picked up little Nevette's school uniform. I want you to take it to Gaston to show your friends and family. I'm so proud of that little boy."

Having said that, Mamie then just stood there. The grin faded. She suddenly realized she might have been overconfident and somewhat self-possessed.

Nona picked up the uniform, smiled and graciously said, "Thank you so much, Mamie. I would love to show this to the folks in Gaston." Knowing, of course, that they may not all be favorably impressed.

The smile returned to Mamie's face as she walked away, singing softly.

≈

The day of departure was exciting. Neb and Luke came from the bakery in the new delivery truck. Luke loaded all the luggage and gifts into the truck. Neb had hired a taxi to transport Nona, the four boys and Mamie. Mamie rode along to help get everyone settled onto the train. The arrival of the entourage at the train station was a sight to behold. Luke was scuttling luggage from the truck to the baggage window. Neb and Nevette were walking together. Nona was directing the two toddlers. Mamie was following, carrying infant Joe.

Everyone, except Luke, boarded the train to help Nona get settled with the four children. Both Neb and Mamie gave Nona a good-bye hug and kiss. When Neb and Mamie exited the train, Neb, very discreetly whispered something in the porter's ear and slipped him a generous tip.

The trip for Nona and the boys went smoothly. It turned out to be an adventure for all five. The train was more comfortable than the one Nona had ridden south some ten years earlier. The porter re-seated them in an area of the car where there were extra, empty seats. The boys had plenty of room to move around or take their naps. Nona laid Joe, the baby, in the seat next to her; where he slept for hours. She had taken books to read to the boys on the train. But the little city fellows were too busy looking out the windows at the country-side to enjoy books. The porter checked on Nona often and showed up at each meal-time to help her escort the children to the dining car.

≈

Even though John and Nona had never met, they had no trouble recognizing each other when Nona stepped off the train in Gaston with four little boys. John was able to fit all the luggage in the back of his black Cadillac. He then situated Nona and the children in the car and off they went to the dairy farm.

John's house at the farm served as headquarters for Nona's trip. Since he had enlarged it, there was plenty of room for both families. He was glad to drive his guests around Gaston for all their other visits. The travelers spent several days at each house until all the family and friends had been seen. Nevette and the two toddlers enjoyed being at John's and Virginia's. They liked playing with their cousins, whom they had just met. John and Virginia now had three little children. The house was filled with activity. But Virginia had more than adequate domestic help. The trip had become a holiday for all involved. The days were packed with chatting and laughter. They reminisced about the economically-challenged years of the past and talked of their gratitude that everyone was doing so well. Everyone had so many questions for Nona about New Orleans and how she and Neb were getting along - questions that had not all been answered in letters through the years.

Several nights into the visit, after all the children had gone to bed, Nona brought out Nevette's school uniform and held it up for John and Virginia to see.

John said, "What the hell is that?"

Nona answered, "Nevette is starting school this fall and this is his uniform."

Looking at the little suit, John snarled, "Why the hell does he need a damn uniform? Doesn't he have enough clothes? If he doesn't have enough to wear, hell, I'll buy him some damn clothes."

Nona was ready for him when she replied, "He's going to a Catholic school, one of the best in New Orleans."

John cut his eyes sharply at Nona and glared at her for a moment. Then he seemed to relax, chewed briefly on his cigar and said, "Well I don't think an education is all that damn important. Just look at me and how well I'm doing. You can bet my children won't be going to any private school and I'm not going to prolong an argument I can't win. But I'm sure you and Neb know what you're doing. I guess it's a good idea."

After that, Nona only showed the uniform to her mother, while Ruby was away at work. She did not mention anything about the school to Ruby, Emma or Ollie. She was afraid it might upset them. And she certainly didn't want to appear braggadocios. She and Neb would educate their boys in the fashion they thought best, regardless of what anyone said or thought. The children were the most important part of their lives and marriage. They were glad for their good fortune in New Orleans. But nothing would ever take precedent over their children.

≈

When the two-week visit came to an end, Nona was somewhat saddened to leave her family and friends. But she was eager to see Neb. They had never been apart before. She was beginning to feel lonely without him and she missed the city. And while John was becoming more and more prosperous and successful in Gaston, she still thought it to be a dismal and depressing little town. The boys had liked playing with their cousins, but they were beginning to want to see their father, and of course, Mamie.

So John loaded the travelers onto the train, tipping the porter in much the same fashion as Neb had. The happy, tired mother and four children headed south. They were going home.

≈

When the train carrying the traveling party pulled into the station in New Orleans they were greeted by the same three who had set them out on their journey two weeks prior. Luke went to the baggage window to collect the luggage. Neb and Mamie boarded the train to help Nona with the children.

It was a glorious sight to behold, everyone trying to hug everyone at the same time. Neb and Nona so glad to see each other. Nevette, Elam and Ray all trying to talk to their father and Mamie at the same time. Mamie hugging the three oldest children while trying to pick up infant Joe. Finally, after much ado, everyone and everything were situated in the taxi and truck.

When they arrived at their home on Erato Street, Luke unloaded the luggage and went back to the bakery. Neb did not go back to work that day, but stayed home to be with his family.

Mamie warmed and served the dinner she had prepared earlier in the day. She cleaned the kitchen and put all the children to bed; all the while humming and singing and hugging babies. Before she left for her little room over the coffee parlor, she served coffee and beignets to Neb and Nona who were sitting on the front porch, talking.

There was so much news to share. Nona told Neb about each family member in Gaston. She told him that her mother was doing fairly well. That her sister, Ruby, was relatively quiet, but polite. She told him how much she enjoyed seeing Emma and Ollie and meeting their husbands and children. And that the two sisters were just as silly as ever. Even though she had not met them previously, she had visited with Neb's three sisters. They now all lived in Gaston. Each sister had sent a hand-written note to her brother. Probably because Nona had suggested it.

She then told Neb about John. "You know he had told us in his letters that he had enlarged the house. It's really nice. And he had also told us that he had bought more land and enlarged the dairy farm. But he doesn't work there very much anymore. He has plenty of help to do that."

She continued, "But did you know that he has gotten into building houses for people and for speculation? He's becoming quite the developer. It's all very impressive. He hadn't mentioned that in his letters. He goes around town in a suit and tie and has a large crew of men working for him. They certainly don't seem to lack for money."

Then Nona leaned over and whispered in Neb's ear, as if someone else was there on the porch listening, "But, our children are smarter than theirs."

Neb just slightly smiled, patted Nona on the knee and said, "Now, now. I'm glad John's doing so well. He always helped take care of me when I was little. I'm grateful to him, and I'd love to see his children."

Neb then got up and went into the house and freshened the two cups of coffee. When he returned, he sat down and said, "Now I need to tell you what I was doing while you were away."

9

Nona, for the first time in two weeks, remembered that Neb had mentioned a new project at work. She looked at him and waited in anticipation, eager to hear what he had to say.

He began, "Uncle Elam has bought even more new equipment for the ice cream business. It was quite an investment, but it's the latest thing on the market. The newly acquired space has turned out to be an ice cream plant. Production and sales are increasing by leaps and bounds. We're already seeing a big increase in profits and expect it to continue."

"Neb, do you think it's wise for him to go into debt like that? Don't you think he's being a little too ambitious?"

"Well, I've learned that he had some money saved. He used a little of it for a down payment on the equipment and financed the remainder of the costs. He has offered the rest of his savings to us for a down payment on a new house. I think that some time in the future, when he gets older or retires, he may want to live with us. I knew about most of the equipment purchases before you went to Gaston for your visit. But, I didn't know about the possibility of a new house. What do you think?"

The news was a lot for Nona to absorb. She thought for a brief moment and said, "Uncle Elam can certainly live with us anytime he would like. This is a nice house, but I guess if he ever wants to move in with us we would need more space."

Neb said, "Well, I don't think it will be any time soon. He says he is perfectly happy for now in his apartment. In the meantime, I thought Mamie could have a room with us. Luke is half grown and that little room over the ice cream parlor is not much for the two of them."

Now, Nona got excited, "Oh, that would be wonderful. I would love it and I know the children would love it. She wouldn't need to ride the streetcar each day. She's like family, anyhow."

"Well, I'm glad to hear you say that. I've already been looking at houses. There's a beautiful house on Bonaparte Street, just off St. Charles Place. Why don't you rest from your trip and then we'll make arrangements to see the house. I think you'll like it."

≈

The house was not among the largest in New Orleans, but it was large. The two-story, white house had a slight Victorian flavor, without too many frills. The front lawn was green and lush with a narrow walk-way that led to eight or nine wide steps that showed off the large front porch. The steps were painted gray, the same color as the floor of the wide porch that went completely across the front of the house. Upon entering the front door, there was a two-story foyer with a curved mahogany staircase to the second floor. The mahogany double doors on the left side of the foyer were pushed into the pockets of the wall, showing off the dining room. The large kitchen was directly behind the dining room. The double doorway on the right side of the foyer led to the living room. At the back of the living room another set of double doors opened into a sitting room. There were four bedrooms upstairs. At the top of the staircase a wide hall had two bedrooms and a bathroom in the middle of the second floor. There was a bedroom at the front of the house that was the largest and certainly intended for the couple of the house. It had a private bath and a space on one side that could serve as a reading area or a very small nursery. The corresponding space at the back of the upstairs had a bedroom with a small, private bathroom that would be perfect for Mamie's quarters.

Nona loved the house. She had never been in anything so big or so nice. But, she found it all somewhat disconcerting. She looked at Neb and asked, "Can we afford a house like this? It all scares me a little bit."

"Don't worry," Neb said. "If at any time it becomes more than we feel we can manage, we can sell it and scale back a little."

Always practical, she thought. That was comforting.

≈

The next several years were golden; filled with happiness and prosperity.

The ice cream business continued to grow.

Two more pregnancies brought two more baby boys, Jack and Charles, into the Kohler household. The days were busy, but glowing. The six little boys enjoyed each others company and got along well together.

The oldest children attended the school at the convent and participated in all the extra curricular activities. There were trips to Audubon Zoo, celebrations for various festivals and parades for religious holidays. They all excelled in their studies and never had to labor with any of their classes or subjects.

Those years were a time of milk and honey for which the Kohlers were grateful and relished every moment. There were sufficient funds to, once again, send money each week to Mama and Ruby in Gaston. The Kohlers had little cause for worry.

≈

But, when the current decade began to wind down late in 1929, the entire nation would be transformed. It would be drained of most everything essential, and the approaching decade would be disastrous beyond belief. Most people did not see it coming and many would not know how to withstand the devastation.

However, the Kohlers also had something else on their minds. Something that concerned them and gave them cause to worry – something that could directly affect their lives and the lives of their loved ones.

10

Early in 1929, Nona began receiving letters from Emma and Ollie telling of employee unrest at Firethorn Mill. The workers were becoming more and more disgruntled. The hours were longer and the working conditions had improved very little in years. Neb and Nona didn't need letters from Gaston to stay abreast of the news. The news of the unrest was splashed across the headlines of the country's biggest newspapers.

Even though a few years earlier a labor union had been voted down by the employees, in the spring of 1929 a major labor union infiltrated the workforce at Firethorn. What ensued became one of the nation's most violent labor disputes in history at one of the world's largest mills.

During the next five or six months, the newspapers gave accounts of brutal rioting. They wrote of the police chief getting killed, and they told of a second death associated with the strike.

Nona was not surprised when she received a thick letter from Ollie. She was afraid to open it. She hoped no one she knew had been killed or injured. It was in small handwriting on four pages of lined note paper. Neb and Nona read it with interest because it gave a different insight into the strike and the events surrounding it.

"Dear folks,

I hope you're both doing well. Things are just a mess here. This strike at the mill has us all worried to death.

A number of union sympathizers have been fired. Some who were only suspected of union allegiance have also been fired. There were surely some who were fired who did not deserve to be. People are scared of losing their jobs. Tom and I are so scared. Everyone in the town is worried in one way or another and worried for whatever reason or gossip that affects them most. So no one ever gave much thought or attention to the mill hand, Sam, who was injured late one night when a bullet hit him in the leg.

You probably don't remember Sam Brown because he worked in the card room. He was a good worker who never gave anyone any trouble. He was not on the side of the union. He was afraid to be. The rumors that it was communist inspired had scared him. To Sam, it was a strange and foreign concept and he wanted no part of it. He was an example of a good and loyal employee. He had visions of becoming a supervisor in the mill. He wanted, more than anything, to provide a good life for his wife and two boys.

You remember that all the machinery in the mill runs twenty-four hours a day and never stops, workers are assigned a particular shift and assignments are rarely changed. Anyone assigned a daytime shift is considered lucky. But, Sam asked to be assigned to a shift that works until very late at night. He said that there would be less competition on that shift and a better chance for a promotion to a supervisory level position.

After about five months into the strike, the riots began to slow down almost to the point of being non-existent. Things had begun to get quiet and the labor union was voted down again. Almost all the mill workers were glad to see the whole ordeal come to an end. Sam was not shy in letting it be known that he was happy with the vote.

Toward the end of September, the late-night whistle blew signaling the end of Sam's shift. He left his position in the card room, spoke to his supervisor as he always did, filed down the stairs with the other workers and went out the front door of the mill. The mill workers, all walking to their homes, were hurrying along. But Sam took time to say hello to anyone willing to speak. Two blocks from the mill, the people began to thin out. After three more blocks and only a block from his family's little, four room, frame mill house, he was walking alone. He wearily turned the corner onto Queen Street.

He was three houses from his home, when the gunshot came from the low hedgerow on the right. The bullet hit his right thigh and he immediately fell to the ground. He knew that the shot came from close range and thought he heard movement in the hedge. He pushed himself up with his left leg and arm and he was able to see somebody running away. He crawled the next hundred or so feet on his left side, dragging his hurt leg. He got to his front door and banged as hard as he could before he passed out.

When Sam regained consciousness in his bed, early the next morning, his wife, Ethel, was by his side. She explained that she found him at the front door and sent the oldest boy, Samuel, back to the mill to fetch Doc Weber, the mill doctor. The doctor gave him a dose of morphine, removed the bullet, set the shattered bone as best he could, cleaned the wound and sewed him up.

Ethel told Sam that Doc said for him absolutely not move and he'll be back later in the morning to see him. When the doctor arrived, he put a crude cast on Sam's leg. Sam was relaxed from the residual morphine and had not thought about much of anything.

Then Dr. Weber stood over him and told Sam to have total bed rest for two weeks and house rest for four more weeks or he'll never be able to use that leg again. If he does what he is told, then he should be able to get around on a limited basis.

Sam's heart began pounding so fast, he later said he thought it was going to leap up through his throat and out of his body. Ethel, Doc Weber, Samuel and Will, the younger son, could not see that. But they all could see Sam's hands begin to shake and tremble uncontrollably. Ten-year-old Samuel started to cry and ran to his daddy's side. Sam looked down at the boy and said he would lose his job at the mill and their mill house. He wondered how he would ever take care of us all.

Over Samuel's sobs, Sam looked up at Dr. Weber and asked how was he going to manage and provide for his family?

Doc said we could worry about that later. Right now he said to just get him well and save that leg.

I don't know what ever became of the Browns. They moved away and no one has seen them since.

I believe all these things to be true. There were several accounts in the local paper and I heard the same story from more than one source.

I can only hope things get straightened out soon. Much love to all and kiss the children for me.

Love, Ollie."

≈

Ollie expounded no further in her letter and did not say that in 1929, a lot of people didn't have jobs or housing and Sam just blended into the ranks. There had been no compensation for his ensuing disability. With the strike coming to an end, people just wanted things to be as they once were. A few concessions had been made and some wages had slightly improved. The workers would settle for that and be happy; knowing that their families were safe and fed. They needed to once more enjoy the environment of their small mill village - the mill village where most all their activities took place.

Every village had a little church and many had several churches serving various denominations. This was where the mill hands worshiped on Sundays, enjoyed the men's fellowship clubs, participated in the women's societies, taught their children bible stories, performed in Christmas pageants and had church picnics in the summers and suppers in the winter. The many churches that had sprung up were not only places of worship, but were the centers for social activities.

Sam Brown, his wife and two sons would not be among those whose lives returned to normal. He would have to leave the mill village and move to a tiny house in the country. He would watch his wife and two boys farm the small piece of land that came with the little, rented house. He would help them as much as he could and when he could. Sometimes the stiff leg or the chronic pain caused by the bullet would inhibit his ability to be a good farmer.

There was one thing Sam was determined not to give up. He made sure his family continued to be faithful members of a church. They would not be able to attend the church in the mill village. They had no way to get there each Sunday. They would find a church close by their house in the country. Except for scratching out a living on their little piece of rented land, the church was their only source of sustenance.

Samuel worked, as laboriously as any ten-year old possibly could to help his family. He could see his father's disappointment and frustration. His heart ached for him. There was little a boy his age could do.

Samuel did come up with a plan. An excellent and honorable plan, he thought. While young Will was a mediocre student, Samuel was bright. He had no trouble making the highest grades in his class at school. He decided to continue working hard on the farm, but work even harder at school. He would find a way to educate himself. He would use his intellect to get ahead in the world and help his father. After all, studying hard and being smart was free. It was something he knew he could do well.

≈

The Browns worked hard, studied hard and went to church in the following tough, brutal years. They would not be the only people struggling to survive. Across the nation masses of people would be without jobs, homes and even food. There would be an economic depression beyond belief - a depression that would drastically engulf the lives of the Kohlers. Any person alive in 1929 would not soon forget that year. The big mill strike would now take a back seat to the depression that would follow. The Kohlers would never forget 1929.

11

The prosperity decade of the 1920's gave most people a false sense of security. This feeling was shattered late in the year in 1929. The Great Depression, as it later came to be called, was believed by most, to be triggered by the stock market crash in October of that year. No one in the country was left untouched. There were no exemptions.

Many believed that the condition was temporary and that recovery was just around the corner. Filled with disbelief, most people expected the thriving economy to return in such short order that they would not be drastically affected.

However, somewhat slowly at first, the euphoria of the '20s began to diminish. As the years would pass, the carefree money spending and money borrowing of the decade would take a downward turn. Many businesses would have to close their doors, especially the merchants of big-ticket items and those that had extended credit.

Even though the ice cream business had begun to dwindle, the bakery and coffee parlor maintained their usual customers in the first few years of the economic decline. While most of the consuming public felt the need to hold onto their money; the small priced purchases didn't seem so imprudent. The cost of a cup of coffee was not too scary. Most anyone could rationalize the price of a loaf of bread and somehow justify the purchase.

Neb and Nona debated ways to reduce their debt in an effort to get by until the crisis passed. Perhaps they should sell their nice home and move into something smaller and less expensive. That idea was soon put aside. The house was home to nine people. And to add to the dilemma, Nona was pregnant again. Another dwelling that would comfortably house them all would cost just as much.

They decided they would find other ways to lower their expenses. They would curtail their shopping trips, various activities and any spending not required for the absolute basics and necessities. Mamie refused to accept her weekly allowance. They would continue to live in the house. Surely, they thought, things would turn around soon.

They remained hopeful for months. The seventh child was born, a son they named Roger. They amused themselves with the birth of another boy. They chuckled and pondered that they would probably never have a daughter.

Uncle Elam came to see the new baby just as he had when the other babies were born. His visits were always enjoyable and the conversation always centered on the baby. After seeing Baby Roger, he left the nursery without saying much and sat in the bedroom where Nona was resting.

Neb got cigars – one for himself and one for his uncle, and pulled up a chair.

Uncle Elam finally spoke, "I know you kids are worried about money. Times are a little tough right now. But, I think we'll get through this. I think everything is going to be alright."

Neb nodded and didn't speak.

Nona said, "I don't think we have many choices at this time."

All three nodded.

Uncle Elam looked at Neb and Nona as if asking for their approval, "Let's not sell anything or make any drastic changes to our lifestyles or businesses. Let's just try to maintain the status quo and ride out the storm."

Again, they all nodded.

12

THE '30s

When the new decade began, the storm worsened.

By 1931, many banking institutions had begun to close their doors and foreclose on homes and businesses. Panic swept the nation.

The customer could no longer justify buying ice cream. People were not willing to pay for such a frivolous luxury; causing Uncle Elam to totally close down ice cream production. He stopped paying rent on that space. No one else could afford to lease it and it just sat empty, except for the refrigeration equipment that no one could afford to buy.

Sales from the bakery and coffee parlor were also diminishing. It saddened Neb and Elam each time another employee had to be let go. A skeleton crew was operating the bakery and coffee parlor.

To say that morale was low at the bakery was an understatement. And, the woeful situation was further complicated when Luke began disappearing for long periods of time.

≈

Luke, now a young man in his 20's, had continued to live in the small room over the coffee parlor. He had, for years, been a dutiful employee and conscientious individual. But now, anyone could see he had begun to change.

This development was evidenced one afternoon when Uncle Elam asked, "Where's Luke? It's time to start cleaning the bakery."

"I don't know," Neb replied.

"Go see if he's upstairs in his room. He may be sick."

Neb went up to the little room, but Luke was nowhere to be found. Neb returned to the bakery and informed his uncle.

Elam said, "That's strange, I know he goes out at night quite often. I can hear him coming and going. But, he's always here during the work day."

No one saw or heard from Luke until the next morning when he showed up for work, smelling of alcohol.

Uncle Elam called him aside, "Son, where have you been?"

"Oh, I was just down at Woodrow's Bar at the docks, with some of my buddies. It won't happen again."

But it did happen again. And again. Sometimes Elam would hear Luke returning to his room in the early morning hours, just in time to go to work in the bakery.

One morning Luke came to work reeking of alcohol. There were cuts and bruises on his face and head. His left eye was almost swollen shut and had begun to ooze blood that was running down his face.

Neb rushed to him and asked, "What happened to you?"

"Oh, it's nothing, Mr. Neb. I just got into a little gambling situation down at Woodrow's. I ended up owing one of the guys that works down at the dock some money. But usually, I win. Please don't mention this to Mama. She'll just worry."

Neb had not previously told Nona of Luke's comings and goings. He certainly hadn't said anything to Mamie about the episodes with

Luke. But he was getting a painfully uneasy feeling regarding the things going on in the young man's life.

When he and Nona were alone in their room that night, with infant Roger asleep in his crib, Neb said, "You know, Nona, I'm worried about Luke. He's been hanging out at the docks and I'm afraid he could get into some serious trouble. I don't really know what to do to help the boy and I don't know if we should tell Mamie or not."

Neb was surprised when Nona said, "Oh, she already knows. Or, at least, kinda knows. He's been trying to borrow money from her."

"Well," Neb continued, "He came in today all beat up. Those men that work the merchant ships and hang around the docks are pretty rough characters."

"I think I should tell her," Nona said. "More than all the things Mamie does for us, I love her as a dear friend and family. I can't keep this from her. He's her son. If one of my sons was in trouble, I'd surely want to know. I'll tell her tomorrow."

≈

As the nation's economy continued to deteriorate, so did the business at the bakery and coffee shop. The economic strings at the Kohler home grew tighter and tighter, and Luke's life continued in a downward spiral.

Due to a lack of customers, Elam was forced to close the coffee parlor; leaving the bakery as the only source of revenue. Elam, Neb and Luke were now the only employees. At least, that was the case, when Luke showed up for work - every other day or so.

When Luke didn't come to work or show up in his room for two days, Neb went home that evening and called Nona into the kitchen.

He said, "Luke's been gone for two days and two nights, I don't know what to do."

Nona thought for a moment and said, "Well. It's late. We'll talk to Mamie in the morning and decide what to do."

No one ever knew if Mamie overheard the conversation or if a mother's intuition activated.

≈

The next morning, Nona awoke. She changed baby Roger and started down the stairs. She thought the kitchen was unusually quiet. Mamie was always bustling around, making coffee and humming to herself at this time of the morning. But, the kitchen was dark. Nona went back upstairs to Mamie's room to check on her. Mamie was not there. She walked across the upstairs hall to her own room where Neb had begun to stir. "Neb, I can't find Mamie. She's not in the kitchen."

Nona put Roger back in his crib, and she and Neb searched the rest of the upstairs rooms. All the little boys were still asleep and Mamie was nowhere to be found. They went downstairs. While Neb looked around the front rooms and checked the front porch, Nona went into the kitchen, turned the light on and started to make a pot of coffee. That's when she saw the note on the table.

She walked over to the table and picked up the note. She was almost afraid to read it and called for Neb.

It was a crudely scratched note that read, "Gone to get my boy."

≈

Neb and Nona stood staring at the note, neither of them knowing what to think. *When did she write it? How long had it been there - since the night before? Where did she go?*

Neb, finally in a tone somewhere between puzzlement and despair, asked, "How much does she know?"

Nona, thinking to herself, slowly said, "I'm not sure. I had told her, just after you and I talked, that he had gotten into a fight. And, she knew he was gambling. That's why he needed money. But she didn't tell me much more."

Then Nona asked the question they were both trying to erase from their minds, "Do you think she went down to the docks last night? It doesn't look like her bed has been slept in. And, why would she stay down there all night?"

Nona's mind was now racing from one thought to another. *Maybe Mamie didn't go to the docks at all. Maybe she was just out walking around. Maybe she didn't want to come in late for fear of disturbing us. Maybe it got late and she stayed over at the bakery in Luke's room.*

"Neb you need to go down to the bakery right now. See if she's there. See if Uncle Elam has heard something."

"I'm going right away. Besides, Elam is probably there by himself and we have to open the bakery. We need the sales."

As Neb turned to walk away, Nevette appeared in the kitchen door carrying baby Roger and said, "He was starting to cry. I think he wants his breakfast."

Nona took Roger in her arms, turned to Neb and said, "Take Nevette with you. He can help you and Uncle Elam. Then send him back here to let me know when you find Mamie. I wish we had one of those telephones."

As Neb left, with Nevette trailing behind, he thought to himself, *I hope I can find Mamie.*

Nona put Roger on the floor and then filled a large pot with water and put it on the kerosene-fueled, cook stove for oatmeal. She knew the five remaining boys would be down soon for breakfast. Since the family had begun to economize, oatmeal and toast had become the standard breakfast fare. Oatmeal was cheap. And Neb always brought home the day-old bread from the bakery.

Whether it was from worry and deep concern over Mamie or the apprehension surrounding their dwindling finances, Nona suddenly felt extremely depressed. She stared at the pot as she stirred the oatmeal. One moment she was thinking, What if he can't find Mamie? She was silently praying, Oh, dear Lord, please let her be safe. The next prayer was, I'm so thankful we have oatmeal and bread. Some people don't have that much or a house like this. Her mind was racing. She couldn't organize her thoughts. Then, she told herself, *I must keep a clear head. This could become a grave situation.*

She was not aware how much time had passed, when she suddenly realized Roger was sitting on the floor crying and five little boys were milling around the kitchen and taking their places at the table.

≈

Neb and Nevette arrived at the bakery and found Elam in the back area, where he was hard and fast at work.

Looking around and realizing he didn't really need to ask, Neb said, "I don't suppose you've seen Luke?"

Elam continued measuring flour. "Nope, don't really expect to. I'm about to believe that boy is hopeless."

Neb inquired, "Well then, I don't suppose you've seen Mamie either?"

That's when Elam's head quickly turned and he saw the worried expression on Neb's face. He stopped what he was doing. "What's wrong?"

"I'm not sure," Neb said. "We can't find Mamie. We think she's been out all night. This is the third day with no sign of that boy." Then with a bit of disgust in his voice, "You know, that really doesn't bother me too much." He was silent for a moment, "But, Nona and I are worried to death about Mamie. She's never done anything like this before."

Neb, shaking his head from side to side, continued, "This is just not like her."

"No, it isn't," Elam said. "What do you think is going on?"

"I don't know. I know Luke has been hanging around down at the docks. Mamie's been really concerned about that lately. Surely, she wouldn't go down there and certainly not at night."

"Neb," Elam said. "You've got to find her. If she's out walking around the city, she's probably okay. But, if she went to the docks, I'd be worried. There're some pretty seamy bars down there. Some of the men that work those ships are just criminals running from the law. I'm going around to the corner and ask the police officer to go down there with you."

"No, no. You're busy here and I'll be fine. I feel really bad leaving you with all this work and customers, too. Nevette is going to stay here and help clean and work the front counter."

Neb left the bakery, caught the proper streetcar and rode to the end of the line. He walked the remaining blocks to the ports.

Large machines and trucks were roaring around the area where the big ships were docked. Men, carrying freight and cargo, were moving up and down the gangplanks, bending under the loads and shouting obscenities.

Leading away from the pier were little narrow streets lined with bars and every kind of entertainment houses imaginable to the twisted mind. Neb left the dock area and began walking up and down the streets. He had to step over and around men lying on the sidewalks, where they were sleeping or in an unconscious state from having drunk too much alcohol. Some had bruises and injuries on their heads and bodies, causing pools of blood on the sidewalks. He felt certain some were dead. He thought to himself, *couldn't someone at least remove the dead bodies?*

He looked at every person or body lying around to make sure none of them was Luke.

Even though it was morning, many of the bars were open. Neb went into each one. The clientele were disorderly and vulgar. He talked to all the bartenders and gave them a description of Mamie and Luke. He even asked some of the drunken sailors, at least the ones who were sober enough to understand, if they had seen anyone looking like the two. He got no satisfactory answers from anyone.

He noticed that most of the bars had little rooms in the back. It didn't take long to learn that was where the poker players and crap shooters were indulging in a pastime that they hoped would buy their next bottle of liquor.

Neb, looking toward one of the back rooms, spoke to the bartender, "Mind if I look around?"

"Go ahead. It's your hide, buddy. But, I can already tell you she ain't back there."

And, she wasn't. Neither was Luke. Neb checked out every back room in every bar. He continued up and down every little street and alleyway, looking at every person.

He began to feel relieved as he thought to himself, *I really don't think they're down here anywhere.*

He decided to go back to the bakery and headed toward the streetcar stop; pausing at the pier to take another look at the big ships. Neb had not seen the seaman that had been watching him from the deck of one of the ships.

As Neb turned and started walking in the direction of the streetcar stop, the seaman yelled down to him, "Hey, you."

Neb stopped and looked up at him.

"Looking for something?" the seaman said.

"Yes, a woman and an older boy. They look like . . ."

But, before Neb could finish his sentence and description, the seaman interrupted and yelled, "Have you tried the morgue?" He then hastily turned and disappeared inside the ship.

Neb knew he would never be allowed to board the ship. He tried to talk to the sailors going up and down the gangplank, but they were totally unaccommodating. He didn't know exactly what the seaman had meant by what he had said. He felt the man knew more than he was letting on. Neb could sense the looks and stares from all the men in the area. He could hear them mumbling to each other. He didn't know what to do next.

He tried to convince himself that everything was going to be fine. He would go back to town and check on Elam and Nevette at the bakery. He was inwardly hoping that Mamie or Luke had turned up there. But all the positive thoughts he could contrive could not blot out the horrible feeling in his gut and the words in his head, *Have you tried the morgue?* He knew what he had to do.

He took the streetcar to downtown, got off and went to the main police station. He looked around until he found the door marked Parish Morgue and went in. He explained to the officer behind the desk why he was there. All the while, hoping the officer would not be able to help him.

But instead, the officer pushed his chair away from the desk, stood up and said, "Mr. Kohler, I think I can end your search. Come with me."

As he walked, Neb followed. The officer continued, "Their bodies were brought in early this morning from down at the docks. You can identify them. We pick up John Does down there all the time. Of course, no one would own up to what really happened. You can file a report, if you want to."

Neb hadn't heard most of what the officer had said. The words, *"Their bodies were brought in . . . Their bodies were brought in . . .,"* were reverberating in his head.

This was by no means his first experience with death. But Neb thought it was, by far, the worst. When the officer pulled the dirty sheets away from the bodies, Neb wondered how anyone could have been so cruel. He had known and seen people who had died from illnesses, but never anything like this. And how could anyone deliberately take the life of an innocent female - a mother trying to help her son.

Later, sitting back at the officer's desk, Neb answered all the questions put before him. He sensed, however, that it was a routine the officer had performed many times before and one that was meaningless. He knew, very well, that no effort would be made to find the perpetrator of this barbaric crime.

≈

He left the morgue, went out the front door and started walking. What should he do? Hours had passed since Neb had left the bakery that morning. He decided he would go back there. He would have to tell Elam the dreadful news. Then he would have to go home and tell Nona. He thought to himself, *she'll be devastated. I don't know how she's going to handle this. I don't know if she can handle this.*

He thought of an innocent mother trying to protect her son. He knew he and Nona would do anything to protect their sons. Their children were their assurance for the fulfillment of a meaningful life.

≈

When Neb got back to the bakery and sent young Nevette on a short, needless errand, Elam stopped shaping the loaves of bread and wiped his hands on his apron. In a very staid voice he said, "Neb, what's wrong? Where's Mamie?"

"She's dead. Luke, too. Apparently she went down to the bars at the docks last night, looking for him. Neither the police nor I know exactly what happened. No one will say."

Elam was silent as he walked across the room and sat down. Bending forward, he clasped his hands across his knees and stared at the floor.

Neb then said, "She, and Luke, had been brutally beaten. My guess is she found Luke and someone was trying to collect on a gambling debt."

The room turned silent. When Elam spoke his voice crackled and the expression on his face was pained. "Neb, this is bad. What are you going to tell Nona and the boys?"

"The boys are little. They'll be alright. Children get over things. It's Nona I'm worried about."

Elam slowly crossed the room and laid his hand on his nephew's shoulder. "Son, I'm so sorry things are going so badly for you and Nona right now. First, the business, now this. You've had some bad blows. You know I'd do anything for you if I thought I could help." He walked to the back stairs and started up to his apartment. "When Nevette gets back, just lock the doors and go on home. Don't bother to clean."

Elam went into his apartment and sat down at the little kitchen table. He dropped his hands into his lap and starred at the floor. He mumbled, "At least you still have your family, your children. I'm afraid I'm getting ready to lose mine."

≈

When they got home, Neb sent Nevette to look after the younger children who were playing in the backyard. He sat with Nona, at the kitchen table, not knowing what to expect. He watched her closely as he talked. He explained everything that had happened and what he had learned. He waited.

She sat silently for a long moment, then reached across the table and took his hand in hers. She said, "We'll be fine. We still have each other, and we have our children."

She got up and poured two cups of coffee from the constantly maintained pot on the stove. She sat back down and passed a cup to Neb. She lifted her cup with one hand, propped her elbow on the table and held her chin in the other hand. She was silent and calm for a few moments. She looked across that table at Neb, who sat staring at his coffee cup. "Now," she finally said, "I'd like you to please go to the convent and ask the sisters to prepare a service for Mamie and Luke for tomorrow. I'll call the boys in and talk to them."

≈

A simple service was held the next day in the City Cemetery. The marginal expenses were paid by the nuns. The only people in attendance were Neb, Nona, the seven little boys, Uncle Elam and a few sisters - mostly the ones that had taught the boys in school.

The many happy, fruitful, glorious years the Kohlers and Mamie had spent together had come to an end, sadly in a pauper's graveyard.

13

Mamie's horrible death was one of the saddest experiences that had occurred in the Kohlers' married life. However, with seven little boys to feed and care for, there was no time, physical energy or mental capacity for grieving. Neb and Nona did have to struggle with the bitterness they experienced as a result of the tragedy. They both agreed that they would not allow it to be all encompassing and they certainly would not pass this badge onto their children.

Besides, other problems were glaring them in the face - problems that would become all encompassing, problems brought about by the extreme lack of money.

Neb and Nona had been poor before. But, they had never been in a predicament like this. They now had a houseful of little children depending on them for food, housing and an education. They decided they would have to sell their lovely home and move into a smaller house. The little boys would have to double-up in their rooms and beds.

Who knows if they waited too long to make that decision? Would trying to sell the house sooner have guaranteed a sale? Given the economic condition of the nation in the mid 1930's, no one could really answer that question. Nevertheless, months passed and no one was even mildly interested in buying the house. Actually no one was interested in buying anything.

They could no longer make payments on the house, meet other household expenses and feed the children. Not unlike many families during that time, they lost their home to foreclosure. They were forced to rent a smaller dwelling in a much less desirable part of town.

This house was even smaller than their first house on Erato Street. The used–to-be-white structure had only four rooms. There were children's beds, bunks and cribs in two of the rooms. Neb and Nona slept in one room and the fourth room was the kitchen. There was one small bathroom on the back porch.

Neb worried about Nona. Her days were long. She took care of seven children. She cooked large quantities of cheap food consisting mainly of grits, oatmeal, dried beans and cornbread. She tried to keep everyone clean and in clean clothes. It was not easy. Quite often a rainy spell or high humidity, which are common in New Orleans, disallowed use of the outdoor clothes line. Laundry for nine people was hanging everywhere inside the little house. The boys by now had so few clothes, it was necessary to wash them often, even if the weather was not always accommodating.

The cramped living spaces, the meager meals and the hard work did not bother Nona and Neb as much as another sacrifice they could not avoid.

The rented house, the only one they had been able to find, was a substantial distance from the convent and school. It simply was not practical for the boys to go to their old school. It was too far to walk and there certainly was no money for streetcar fare. The children had to be enrolled in the public school not far from the house. Nona knew it was a good school, probably better than the ones she had attended in Gaston. But, she also knew it did not offer the same educational acceleration as the convent school.

So in addition to her many daily chores, she made sure that each night the boys did more than their required homework. There were extra library books to read, advanced math problems to solve and additional geography to be learned.

Nona did all these things for the children, but she also did them for herself. She relished knowing that she was getting an education also. She learned as the boys learned. It didn't require any money and she felt that it was a near luxury. Perhaps it also served as an escape or some sort of diversion. It certainly helped keep her mind off the unyielding financial burden that continued to germinate.

≈

Approaching the mid '30s, Neb and Uncle Elam finally accepted the inescapable truth that the bakery could no longer generate enough revenue to support two families. Uncle Elam had for a time only held back enough income for his own lean existence. But, there still was not enough left for Neb and Nona to get by. Neb would have to take to the streets and look for a job, along with the thousands and thousands of other men without work.

The Kohlers considered going back to Gaston. But in the letters from Nona's mother, John, Emma and Ollie, they realized that conditions there were no better than in New Orleans. There simply were no jobs. According to the newspapers there probably was no where in the nation they could go that would make even the minutest difference in their plight.

And as fate, whether worldly or spiritual, would have it, Nona was pregnant again.

≈

Neb pursued every job possibility he could uncover. Quite often he stood in long lines with hundreds of other out-of-work men, knowing full well there would be no work available. Finally, he got a job with one of the construction crews on what would become the Huey P. Long Bridge. He had worked there for one week and brought home his first paycheck on the day the baby was born. Of course it was a boy, named Ed.

With the birth of another child, the physical exhaustion and mental anxiety for Neb and Nona were becoming overwhelming. In early 1936 after the bridge was completed and opened, most of the work crews were laid off. Neb was un-employed again. It was then that the Kohlers realized they could not continue paying rent on the little four-room house. Neb, Nona, the seven little boys and new baby would literally and physically be on the streets.

They would have to go back to Gaston. They could stay with family and friends. No one person had enough room for all of them. They would have to be lodged in different houses. At least, they would all have shelter. Even though Neb had not said the words and thoughts aloud, he was hoping John might be able to help him find some kind of work - any kind of work that might help him provide for his family.

≈

After agonizing discussions and much soul-searching, the decision was made. They would pack as many belongings as practical to carry on the train and leave the city they loved, the city where they had spent almost twenty, wonderful years.

On the day before departure Neb went to the bakery. Uncle Elam was there making the few loaves of bread he hoped to sell that day. He was now an old man, moving slowly around the work area.

Even though Neb had gone there to talk, he joined in and helped the old gentleman with the preparation and baking.

"Elam," Neb finally said, "I'm going to have to take Nona and the boys back to North Carolina. I don't know what else to do."

"I understand," Elam solemnly said. "I've known for sometime this day and this discussion were coming."

Neb added, "I want you to come with us,"

"Oh, no, no, no. I'll be fine here. I've got my little apartment and I do enough business each day to buy a few groceries. I still have a few old friends up and down the street. I'll be fine. I just wish there was more I could do for you. I'm going to miss you, but we've all got to think of those children. It's meant a lot to me having you and Nona with me for so long. I feel like the boys are my grandchildren." He chuckled softly and said, "You know some of them are already half-grown. Nevette will be finishing high school soon. I expect you to let me know when he does."

After delaying the inevitable longer than practical, Neb left the bakery. He still had to go to the train station to buy the tickets for tomorrow's journey and then back to the house to help Nona pack.

≈

When he stepped up to the ticket window at the station, he was reminded of the young man who had been twenty years younger and so eager to buy tickets for his exciting trip. When he once again learned he didn't have enough money. Neb was not eager to buy tickets for this particular trip. But the memory of some twenty years ago was vivid in his mind. He remembered the day before his wedding. He told himself that he had managed once before and he could do it again. Even with a few half fares for the toddlers and a free ride for Baby Ed, he still did not have enough money to buy tickets for the entire family. He bought as many as he could.

He was still two tickets short. He and Nevette would have to stay behind. The thought of sending Nona off alone with seven little boys frightened him. *Perhaps,* he thought, *I should send Nevette with her and keep one of the other children with me in New Orleans. No, that was not a good idea. Nevette is older and might be able to pick up odd jobs around the city that would put us closer to earning enough money for those last two tickets.*

Neb left the train station, went back to the little house and found Nona stuffing every suitcase, satchel and available bag with every piece of clothing she could find. By this time their belongings had dwindled. Some of the hand-me-downs had been passed down until they were becoming thread bare. But she had to take them. It was all they had. She found room for a few keepsakes, a few photographs and the family Bible. She was exhausted and the news that Neb and Nevette would not be going with her and the other boys at this time was disheartening. But, she was able to convince Neb that she would be alright.

She said she would ask John would to meet her at the train station and everything would be fine.

≈

Perhaps everything would be fine in Gaston. No one really knew. Things certainly were not fine the next morning at the train station. Nona felt relatively sure she would never see New Orleans again. Something she would have to accept. She could not bear the thought of being away from Neb and separating the family. No one really knew how much time would pass before Neb and Nevette could get to

Gaston. As she stood with Baby Ed in her arms, she was barely able to tell Neb and her first born son good bye without crying.

As much as anything he had ever done, Neb hated sending Nona off alone with seven children to care for. And of all places, Gaston, the place he disliked so much. He knew he had to do it. He had to consider Nona and the kids. He knew they would be better off near family. Regardless of the unknown surrounding their future living conditions and well being, family and old friends offer support and comfort. He knew his wife and children would be safe there, something he could not know for sure if they stayed on in New Orleans.

As the train pulled away, Neb and Nevette began walking back to the bakery. They would have to bunk in with Uncle Elam or simply live in and around the bakery until they could raise enough money to buy more train tickets. Living in Gaston had been bad. But Neb had never been as sad in Gaston as he was on this day in New Orleans.

Nona watched out the window of the train as they walked away. The self-sufficient little boys found seats around her and settled in for the trip. She was glad they could take care of themselves and look after each other. For as she sat holding Baby Ed, she felt her inner being crumbling and she could no longer hold back the tears.

≈

When Uncle Elam heard the bell on the front door of the bakery jingle, he started walking toward the front area. "Do you need a loaf of bread?" He walked into the front room and saw Neb and Nevette coming in. "What the," his voice drifted away. "What's going on?" He finally said, "Are you two alright?"

"Yeah, we're fine," Neb answered. "I realized after I left here yesterday that I didn't have enough money for all the train fares and I was too busy helping Nona to come back by here and let you know. I had to send her and the other boys on to Gaston alone." He then woefully added, "I won't have any way of knowing if they get there safely. She'll write. But a letter will take a few days to get here."

Neb continued, "You know this is bad. We don't even know for sure where they're all going to stay. God, I hated to send her off like that with all the children."

"Now, now, Nona and those boys will be fine. They're very resourceful. You needn't worry about them. In the meantime, you two can stay upstairs with me. Or you could sleep in Luke's old room over the coffee parlor. It's no longer my space. But, it's just sitting there empty. The landlord will never know any better."

"No," Neb said. "That wouldn't be right. It's no longer our property and I won't do that. We'll stay upstairs with you. I'll sleep on the sofa and Nevette can sleep on the floor."

"That's fine. Tomorrow we'll see if we can earn some money for those tickets. I'll make extra bread. Perhaps you can go around town and sell it. You know there's an old pushcart out back you can use. Nevette, you can go to all the merchants up and down the street and see if you can get some odd jobs and earn a few cents." Elam continued, "Try not to worry. The look on your face concerns me."

14

GASTON

Nona's train trip to Gaston was not the joyous occasion it had been some years prior. This was not a social visit. This trip was an act of desperation. The porters were kind and chatted with all the little boys. But there were no trips to the dining cars and no books to read. And, Nona was certainly not in the mood to entertain children.

The little fellows sat quietly in their seats and ate from the bag of sandwiches that had been prepared for the trip - sandwiches made of nothing more than sliced bread and cheap luncheon meat. Charles said, "Mama, are you alright?"

Joe took Charles by the arm, "Come sit with me. She's just a little upset."

They were all glad when the trip was over and happy to see Uncle John waiting for them at the station. All the boys gave their uncle a hug, even the ones he had never seen. John gave Baby Ed a long, extended look. Nona explained the situation with the train fares and that Neb and Nevette planned to join them just as soon as there was enough money for the tickets.

As the crew of little children ran ahead to the car, John walked with Nona and watched and asked, "Damn, Nona. Don't you and Neb know when to stop? Or maybe you don't know where the hell these little fellows come from."

Nona chuckled and said, "Oh, we know alright."

But then more seriously, she stated, "Hopefully, there will not be anymore children for us. Especially with things the way they are now. I don't know if Neb and I will ever get back on our feet. It's been pretty rough."

"Well," John said, "Let's just get this crew out to the house and get something to eat, and try to find a place for everyone to sleep."

"Oh, John, we can't all stay there. There are too many of us. We can't impose on you and Virginia like that. Besides, you have four children of your own."

"Hell, I'm not letting you separate these little boys. At least we have plenty of quilts for pallets. They can sleep on the damn floor. I'll drive you around later in the week to see your Mama and Ruby."

After John had bought his first car years ago, he had always made a practice of getting a new car each year. However, the car he was driving today had some age on it. But it was big and everyone was able to fit into it. The little boys sat on the older boy's laps. The few belongings Nona had brought on the train were all put in the big trunk. They then headed off to the dairy farm to greet Aunt Virginia and their cousins.

Signs of the depression were evident at the farm. It was still making a little money, but had not experienced much growth in several years. The construction business John had started years earlier was also making a little money. But very few people could afford to make improvements to their homes and very few businesses could afford to expand. However, he had long ago paid off the debt on the farm. While his income was not what he would like it to be, he was managing to get by and provide for his family.

John was obviously not as prosperous as he had been some years earlier. But his financial state and living conditions were far better than most. Virginia did not have the servants she had once had. There was an elderly black couple living on the premises to help with the house keeping chores and the various barn and cow requirements. They worked there without pay; probably because they really didn't have anywhere else to go. There was ample food for everyone. It was simple farm food and all the New Orleans Kohlers relished every bite.

At night there were wall-to-wall children sleeping on pallets. All the little cousins loved it. The older ones were not quite so enthusiastic over the arrangement. But, they knew they had no choice and accepted their plight graciously.

Nona was grateful for the hospitability. But, she was extremely concerned over how long they would have to stay at John's. She wondered constantly how long it would be before Neb and Nevette could join them. Of course, the big question was what they all would do when Neb did arrive. She immediately sent a letter to Neb in care of Uncle Elam at the bakery.

≈

Five days later Neb walked into the bakery; after having pushed his wooden cart up and down the streets of New Orleans trying to sell bread. He had not made much money. Even Nevette doing odd jobs, had made a few cents more then Neb.

"Neb," Elam said, excitedly waving something in his hand, "You got a letter from Nona."

Neb smiled as he read of their safe arrival and living arrangements. They were all doing well, but missed him terribly. The letter didn't say much more. It didn't have to. He knew they were safe and the statement of missing their husband and father was motivation enough. In the next week Neb became the most aggressive street vendor in the city. He smiled and chatted with prospective customers and sold bread in abundance. By the end of that week he and Nevette had raised enough cash for their two train tickets to Gaston.

Nevette, a tired teenager, was able to sleep through a good portion of the trip. Neb had too much on his mind to sleep. He had hoped he would never have to live in Gaston again. Now he was on his way back there. Admittedly, it gave him a slight sense of relief. At least it was better than being on the streets of New Orleans. But he worried and wondered what he could do in Gaston to provide for his family. He thought to himself, *I'll go to work in a mill, if I have to.*

≈

John met Neb and Nevette at the station. They had not seen each other in years. After a long embrace, the emotions they were feeling were definitely mixed. They were certainly glad to see each other, but not under these circumstances. They all made their way to the car and Nevette jumped into the back seat. The two men rode in the front and talked.

"How are Nona and the boys?" Neb asked.

"They're all fine," John answered.

"How's Virginia?"

"She's fine."

"How are your four children?"

"They're fine."

"Farm doing good?"

"It's fine."

After a long silence Neb finally said, "John, I don't know what we're going to do. I have to look for a job and that's going to be difficult enough. In the meantime, I have to find somewhere for all of us to live. I really don't know how or where to start. I would hate to have to break the family up and put the children around in different houses. But I don't know what else to do."

"Oh hell, Neb, you can't do that. Do you have any money or anything left?"

"Not a cent."

"Well," John said. "I've thought about it. I know where there's an empty log cabin. It's pretty sparse. But at least you'd all be together. It's on Mr. Clemmer's farm. He's a man I know. We've traded some cows. I reckon he has about fifty or so acres out in the country. The cabin is back in the woods about a half-mile from his farmhouse. It's been sitting there empty for a hell of a long time. I asked him about it and he said you can use it if you want to. Just pay him when you can."

Neb, somewhat encouraged said, "That sounds good. For now I'll have to take it."

John continued, "Don't be too hasty. Here's the really bad part. The damn thing doesn't have electricity or running water. There's a spring about fifty yards away that's clean. But that's about it."

"You know, John, we all managed under those conditions when we were growing up in McLean. We didn't have electricity or running water then. Nona and I will just have to do the best we can."

"Well, since you'll be living out in the country, I've got a mule and wagon I'm not using. And I can spare a cow. Virginia can pull together some old quilts and bedding. I'll ask her to pack up a few staples from the kitchen to help you get started."

Neb nodded in gratitude and said, "If it's alright with Nona, we'll move out to the cabin tomorrow and then I can start looking for a job."

John added, "I've got a couple of small construction projects going. I could use some help on them if you're interested. It's mostly digging ditches right now and I don't know how long they will last, but I might as well pay you as someone else. That is, if you're interested."

"Right now I'm interested in any job I can get. I'd even go to work in one of the mills."

"Well that's not going to happen. They're not hiring right now. Everybody around here knows that. This damn depression has slowed down everything."

Neb said, "Have you mentioned any of this to Nona?"

"Not a word."

"Good, I'll tell her when I see her."

John then added, "At least it's spring. There's still time to put in a garden. Nevette and the older boys can take care of it. Hell they're old enough to see to the mule and cow, too. You know, I probably can spare a few of those laying chickens. That'll help."

Neb couldn't help but chuckle as he said, "Those boys are used to streetcars, grocery stores and street vendors. The only animals they have seen were at the zoo. But they're smart and willing to learn and work. I'm sure they'll be taking care of things in no time."

≈

That night after supper, Neb and Nona sat on the porch of the farmhouse while John and Virginia bedded down all the children. Nona listened as Neb told her about the cabin and the possibility of working on one of John's construction sites. It all sounded as depressing to her as it had to Neb earlier. But they both agreed that they had no other options. This was the right thing to do for the entire family.

Virginia was up early the next morning and prepared a huge breakfast of pork chops, fried potatoes, eggs, biscuits and homemade preserves. After the sixteen people were fed, she packed bags of coffee, dried beans, flour, sugar, cornmeal and grits. She included a can of lard and the remainder of the eggs the chickens had laid that morning. She made a big bundle of quilts. The men loaded everything on the wagon and tossed in an axe and a few farm tools that John could spare. The mule was hitched to the front of the wagon and the cow was tied behind. Nona loaded all the boys and their belongings in the wagon. With John's directions and Neb driving the mule, they set out for the cabin. It was a heart-rending sight. Very unlike a typical scene of a few years earlier, when Mamie took little boys in starched white shirts and uniforms to private schools and served coffee to Nona and Neb on their pretty front porch.

The roads were crudely paved and bumpy. The younger boys were enjoying themselves, as if the ride were a pleasure trip or some sort of amusement ride. The older boys knew better. They knew this was an appalling situation and wondered what lay ahead for them.

As they jogged along in the wagon, Nona spoke to Neb, "You know, early on I wondered if it was wise for Uncle Elam to have bought so much refrigeration equipment and invested so much money in the ice cream business. Everything was going along okay and we were doing just fine. But in the long run, I don't think it would have mattered. I think the outcome would have eventually been the same. We would have lost everything. The amount of the investment wouldn't have mattered. Hell, people can't even afford to buy bread."

Neb burst out laughing, "Either you've been around John far too long or you're becoming a tough little lady."

Nona laughed back, "I think it's the latter. John's language doesn't bother me. I decided I'm going to have to be a tough little lady with what we're up against right now. You know a cabin in the summer doesn't seem so bad. But if we're still there when winter comes, it could become difficult. This is not New Orleans. I remember Mama's and Ruby's frame house in the winter with that little wood burning stove. It was cold. Well, this is a cabin with a fireplace. It'll be even colder in the winter. An iron cook stove would help keep it warm. Does it have a cook stove?"

"I don't know," Neb answered.

≈

The wagon trip took over three hours. The oldest boys walked most of the way to lighten the load for the mule. It was rough and tiring. Neb and Nona were glad when they reached the Clemmers' farmhouse. They knew they only had a half-mile farther to go. They found the trail through the woods that led to the cabin. The old wagon trail had not been traveled in years. The shrubs that bordered the wagon path were overgrown. The opening through the trees was just wide enough to get the wagon through and tree branches brushed against the Kohlers' faces. The wagon creaked when the wheels rolled over a tree root or hole. Finally all the boys, except

Baby Ed, got off and started walking. It took over thirty minutes to make the half-mile trek through the woods to the clearing. The sun was bright when the wagon left the cover of the trees. The oldest boys had run ahead of the wagon and stood staring at the cabin when the wagon carrying Neb, Nona and Baby Ed emerged from the woods. The cabin stood in the middle of a clearing. It was made entirely of rough-hewn logs. Or, so it appeared. Most of the sides of the structure were covered with ivy and vines. The entire family stared at the dwelling, not knowing what to think or say.

Finally, Joe, his voice filled with disbelief, remarked, "I've never seen anything like this, except in history books in school. Are we at the right place? Are we really supposed to live in that? It looks like a pioneer's cabin or something Abraham Lincoln lived in."

"Oh, now boys," Nona said, trying to maintain a cheerful voice. "We'll all be together and we'll be fine. Let's look inside."

Neb took the baby in one arm and helped Nona climb down from the wagon and everybody went inside.

It looked smaller inside than it had from the outside. There were only two rooms with a pass through fireplace. It was dark and dreary and felt very damp. The place was hanging with cobwebs and dust. There were wooden racks built on the walls to hold bedding. When they all looked down, they were met with the most shattering blow of all. Their hearts sank. They felt sick. There was no floor built into the cabin. It was sitting on dirt. Nona felt her body sinking as if her legs had given way under her. She reached out to steady herself in the doorway. Her voice ringing of desperation, she said, "Neb, what are we going to do? Do you really think we can live here? Can we live in a cabin with dirt floors?"

≈

Before Neb could think or say a word, there was a commotion outside. All the Kohlers stepped back out into the light and saw a family on a wagon. The mother and father were both large, big boned, tall people. The two teenage children and the two younger children appeared to be just as strapping. The three oldest were girls and the youngest was a plump, baby-faced boy.

While Neb, Nona and the Kohler boys stood staring, the father spoke first, "We're the Clemmers. We live in the farmhouse you just passed up the way. We're just plain, ole country folk and we're glad to have you. This is my wife Mrs. Clemmer. These kids are ours, Mary Faye, Annie Sue, Frances and Dan."

Mrs. Clemmer climbed down from the wagon with no trouble, even though both hands were holding pots and plates. In a soft, but penetrating and high-pitched voice, Mrs. Clemmer announced, "I brought a pot of beans, some biscuits and a chocolate cake for your supper. Sloan, that's Mr. Clemmer's name, has a cook stove on the back of the wagon for you. And we're all here to help you clean this place up. There's a dilapidated old barn over there on the other side of those trees. Sloan and Neb can repair it and make a place for the cow and mule. There are some buckets on the wagon. You're going to need them to carry water from the spring. Now, you children get the buckets and start carrying water up here to the cabin and let's start cleaning."

Even though Mrs. Clemmer spoke with authority and assurance, she was smiling all the while; as if all the to-do was an every day occurrence. The Kohlers had been standing still in their tracks as if their feet were glued to the dirt beneath them. Their eyes were wide as they stared at the Clemmers. They all simply said, "Thank you," and started moving in accordance with the matriarch-drill sergeant's instructions. Mrs. Clemmer went inside the cabin and began dusting down cobwebs while she merrily sang and talked. "Tomorrow's Sunday, y'all will have to come to our house for Sunday dinner after church. I think three or four fried chickens should be enough for the two families. You can go to church with us if you don't already have one of you own. We're Presbyterian. But the Browns, on the other side of the hollow, are Methodist. They really love their church. You might want to go with them. You know, I wasn't thinking. Y'all got a lot to do around here. Maybe you'd rather stay home and get things done and just rest. But we still want y'all to come for dinner and we can get better acquainted. We've only got the one son, but he's got some old clothes he's not wearing that will probably fit one of your boys. You sure do have a lot of boys. Well, maybe you'll have a girl someday. Do you want a girl?"

Nona thought to herself, *that woman sure does talk a lot. I haven't seen her take a breath. She must be breathing through the pores of her skin. For a moment I almost forgot about the dirt floors. But I'm certainly glad they're here.* When Mrs. Clemmer stopped talking, Nona jumped in, "No, we really don't expect to have a girl and hope we don't have anymore children. We can't afford to feed the ones we already have and we're perfectly happy with all boys."

Mrs. Clemmer started talking again. "Oh, God always provides a way, in some form or fashion. By the way, my name is Johnette. I was named after my daddy. Have you ever heard of anybody naming a baby girl after its daddy? Well, my folks did. But everybody calls me Mrs. Clemmer. And, everybody calls Mr. Clemmer by his whole name, Sloan Clemmer. Now, ain't that strange? But, that's what our kin and everybody at church calls us, Mrs. Clemmer and Sloan Clemmer." Finally returning to the subject of the moment, Mrs. Clemmer then said, "Your family's going to be just fine. Those look like hard-working boys. They'll be a big help to you and Mr. Kohler."

Nona, who had begun dusting the racks that would hold the bedding, thought to herself, *we don't want our boys to have to help us; we want to help our boys.* Both she and Neb knew that while the eight boys were a huge responsibility, they were all and everything they had in the world. Perhaps someday, the boys would be their salvation and saving grace. But for now, all she knew was that they were the most important part of their lives. Asset or not, their boys were sacred.

Nona's thoughts were interrupted when she heard the sounds of the hammers and saws from the barn. Sloan Clemmer and Neb were busy repairing the old barn and getting to know each other. The children of both families had begun bringing water from the spring. Mrs. Clemmer had put the oldest children to work scrubbing the walls, the table and the few other fixtures in the cabin.

The various chores and cleaning procedures had continued for several hours, with all the children and adults getting to know each other, when Mrs. Clemmer announced, "Now, you men get that cook stove off the wagon and put it in the cabin. Then cut a hole in the wall and run that pipe through it for good exhaustion. Mary Faye, you're my best milker. You milk that cow. Mrs. Kohler's going to need that milk for supper tonight. Besides, it's time and that cow needs milking. While you're at it, show these Kohler boys how to milk a cow. I'll bet they don't know how. Then we got to get back to the house. I've got to kill those chickens and get them ready for tomorrow's dinner. Then we've got to read the Sunday School lesson and get ready for church tomorrow. Francis, did you iron your dress yet?"

≈

"Mama, Mama, I want to go. Can we please go? Mama, are you awake?" Jack was tugging at his sleeping mother.

Charles chimed in, "I want to go, too. Frances said we could go with them."

Nona awoke, not knowing where she was. As she gained her composure, she looked around and realized she was in the cabin, after having spent the first night there.

Ray, probably because he was older, walked up and said, "Well, I don't think we should go. There's too much that needs to be done around here. Besides, we don't even know if we want to be Presbyterian"

That's when Nona remembered it was Sunday and the Clemmers had invited them to go to church. The night before had been pleasant enough. It had been a comfortable, spring evening. After the new neighbors left, the log cabin and surroundings had looked somewhat better. The family had enjoyed the supper Mrs. Clemmer had prepared for them. Everyone was tired and had rested well. However, before bedtime, Neb and Nona had walked around outside the cabin and out to the barn, talking. They knew the cabin was a horrible living arrangement. They knew it would require significant adjustment for the whole family. Each had tried to console the other. They talked about their arrival in New Orleans almost twenty years ago when they had nothing. Eventually they had a wonderful life there. They agreed they would work and create another good life for their family. However, everything was so different now. The '20s were over. The entire nation had been in a downward spiral for years. Starting over would not be anything like starting out in New Orleans. Their dilemma seemed almost inextricable. To add to the complexity, they now had eight children. Their situation was so dire they could only concentrate on keeping the youngsters fed and clothed. Thinking about anything more than these necessities seemed totally unreasonable. As they walked Nona had tried not to allow her disappointment show. She had had such auspicious dreams and hopes for the boys. She had especially wanted their children to have a good education, even before she and Neb ever had children. She remembered the first time she had seen the convent in New Orleans and had hoped their children could go there to school. Now she could only hope that they could keep them all fed and sheltered. Upscale, private schools would no longer be a part of their lives. They now lived in log cabin with dirt floors. The arrangement was only a step above camping out. Given their current state of affairs, she couldn't allow herself to think about private schools and such. She had to focus on surviving. She had to make the best life possible for her children and she had to nurture their spirit and character. She would set an example and teach them patience and tolerance. She would be the one to teach them love and respect for themselves and others. Neb possessed all the qualities that made him an excellent disciplinarian, a characteristic that would teach the boys to excel. She knew he would find a way to provide for them. But she also knew she would have to be the strong one. She would be the leader.

She sat up in the bed and looked around the room.

Having just awakened, the younger children were wandering around not doing much of anything. Nevette and Joe had found the proper pot and were managing to make a pot of coffee.

Nona threw her feet off the edge of the bed, and said, "Neb, you take Nevette and Ray out to the barn and milk the cow and find something to feed that mule. Joe, go through all those bags and find something for everyone to wear. I'll make a pan of biscuits. After breakfast, we are all going to get dressed and walk up to the

Clemmers' house and go with them to church. If we decide we want to choose another church later, we will. But, today we're going to church."

≈

It was not until the Kohlers arrived at the Clemmers' house that beautiful, spring morning that Sloan Clemmer and Mrs. Clemmer realized that there was not enough room in the car for both families to go to church all at once. However, it was still early. Sloan Clemmer would have to make two trips in his dilapidated, beat up car. He said he was glad to do it and took his family first, along with Nevette and Elam. He would drive right back for the rest of the Kohlers. Everyone would get to church on time. They all laughed that it would also take two trips to get the entire assemblage back home after church.

The pretty little church, about four miles away, was constructed of large, light brown mud brick with a cedar shingle roof. It sat on a knoll at the foot of a small mountain. The grounds of the church and all the trees on the knoll and mountain were popping with shades of green. Even the ivy that was intermittently growing up the outside walls of the church was bright green. The dogwood trees on the side of the mountain were glowing white with blooms. The azaleas that outlined the front of the little church were emerging in pink colors. The Kohlers thought it was a most picturesque, beautiful sight and very different from the city churches in New Orleans.

All the Kohler children loved Sunday School and were made to feel welcome. The oldest boys said they were reminded of their convent schools in New Orleans. The Kohlers sat directly behind the Clemmers at the eleven o'clock service and filled the entire pew. After the service and speaking to the preacher at the door of the church, all the parishioners stood around the front lawn to chat and visit. Many of them would not see each other again until next Sunday. When the time came to disperse and head home for Sunday dinner, church members began showering the Kohlers with gifts and goods they had brought from their homes. There were all kinds of staples for the kitchen, jars of canned vegetables and fruit, farm tools that could be spared and hand-me-down clothes that children had outgrown.

Nona looked at Mrs. Clemmer and asked, "How did everyone know we had moved here?"

"Oh, Sloan Clemmer began to spread the word yesterday morning. Then I told some folks this morning when I got here early. They ran back home and got stuff. They're like that out here in the country."

Neb shook all the men's hands in gratitude.

When everyone got quiet, Nona was very graciously thanking the entire group of church members for their kindnesses. As she spoke, Ray was persistently tapping his mother on the shoulder. Finally, Nona turned and very kindly said, "Yes, Ray. What is it?"

Ray, in a voice so audible it could be heard across the entire churchyard, said, "But I don't want to be a Presbyterian."

For a few seconds the silence was deafening. Nona really didn't know what to do or say. Suddenly the whole church congregation broke into laughter. Mrs. Clemmer walked over, put her arm around Ray's shoulder, chuckled aloud and said, "Son, you don't have to become a Presbyterian. We do things like this for lots of people, all the time." Then laughing even louder, she said, "Even the Baptists."

When everyone had stopped laughing the second time, she asked, "Besides, how do you know so much about the Presbyterians?"

"I read a lot," Ray said. "I know about all the faiths."

"Oooh!" said Mrs. Clemmer, with a smile and her eyebrows slightly raised.

≈

Sunday dinner at the Clemmer house was fun for everyone. After the kitchen had been cleaned, the adults sat on the front porch in rocking chairs and talked and told amusing stories from their pasts – pasts that were very different. The two sets of children found a rope and hung an old tire from a tree down in the hollow near the spring. This was a different kind of entertainment for the Kohler boys whose playtimes had been largely spent in the park in New Orleans. For a while everyone's worries were erased. There was no repining over trying times. It was one of the most relaxing and enjoyable days the Kohlers had had in sometime. Even Nona tried to clear her mind of all they were up against and what she feared lay ahead for them.

When it was time for Sloan Clemmer and Dan to feed the farm animals, the Kohlers went back to their cabin. They had not been there long when Ray ran into the house and told his mother, "We have company. I think it's the Brown's. Their two boys played with us this afternoon in the hollow. Remember Mrs. Clemmer said they are Methodists. I want to be a Methodist."

"Ray, I told you this morning, we'll see to that later," Nona informed him.

Joe, the most cynical of all the children, jumped into the conversation, "Well, I didn't think those Brown boys were so great. The older one is a smarty-pants and the younger one is dumb."

"Now, now boys. We're going to visit with our guests. I know you'll be polite. You always are."

Neb and Nona met the Browns outside the cabin and introduced themselves. The Browns said their names were Sam and Ethel. The boys that had already gone off to play in the hollow with the Kohler boys were Samuel, the older and Will, the younger. Samuel was just a little older than Nevette, but still in high school. Will appeared to be between ten and thirteen years old. It was hard to tell. Physically he looked to be thirteen or older. But, he acted somewhat childish and unruly. Sam Brown, the father, walked with a pronounced limp.

Ethel had brought an egg custard that Nona sliced and served to the adults along with a pot of coffee. The four adults sat on the grass outside the cabin and chatted.

It was not long before the conversation came around to the subject of Sam's leg and his difficulty walking. Nona said, "You know, about ten years ago while we were living in New Orleans, we received a letter from a friend here in Gaston. She told us about an employee at Firethorn Mill, a Mr. Brown, that had gotten shot in the leg during the strike. Could that have been you?"

Sam said, "Yeah, yeah, that was me. It's been about ten years since I took that bullet. It was during that big union strike and there was a lot of bad stuff going on. We never found out who did it. It's caused my family a lot of grief. I've never been able to work anywhere else since then, except out here around the farm. I have some good days and bad days and can't really hold down a job. We manage as best we can on our little farm. The boys help a lot. 'Course, Samuel says he wants to go off to college. Then I'll just have Will to help out. I haven't figured out yet how Samuel thinks he can go away to school. Ethel and I sure can't afford to send him. He says his grades are so good he can go to college on some kind of scholarship. I guess we'll see,"

Neb and Nona explained that they had worked at that mill many years ago before they got married. They also said they remembered the big strike very well, having read about it in the newspapers while in New Orleans.

The Browns stayed 'til nearly dark. Before they left for home, Ethel said, "We'd love for you to come with us to church next Sunday. We go to the little Methodist Church just up on the main road. If you don't have a car right now, you can walk there this time of the year. It's not too far. Anyhow, the boys will see each other during the week and we'll talk and decide. And oh yeah, we've got some extra tomato plants and okra seeds we don't need this year. I'll send them over later this week. I assume you're going to put in a garden."

≈

After the Browns left, Neb and Nona continued sitting outside on the grass, sipping coffee. They talked about the nice day they had enjoyed. They discussed their new neighbors and friends. They laughed about the incident with Ray over the Presbyterians. Nona said, "I guess we should try the Methodist Church next Sunday. I don't want Sloan Clemmer making so many trips each Sunday just so we can go to church. We can, at least for the next six months or so, walk to the Methodist Church. We'll worry about next winter when it comes." Nona continued, "Neb, we really do need to have a garden. If we get it started, the boys can take care of it. I can show them how. We probably need to can some things this summer for next winter. But we don't have any jars. There's so much we need, I'd hate to spend money on jars. Well, I'll figure something out. Right now we've just got to get some money and more food in this house.

Everyone was generous with their gifts today, but that stuff won't last long."

Neb agreed, "It is time to plant a garden. I think I can borrow a plow from John or Sloan Clemmer and pull it behind the mule. I'll have to get the plot cleared and plowed. I know I can't do it tomorrow. I'm going to try to find a way into town. John's building a new loading dock at Myrtle Mill. He's going to pour the concrete tomorrow. I'm sure he can use my help and I can make a few dollars. When the truck dumps that concrete, you have to be there ready to work it and stay with it as long as necessary. I may be gone all day. You'll be alright here out here, won't you?"

"Oh, sure."

"I'll get that plot ready this week."

Before they could continue their conversation, Roger ran up to them with a worried look on his face. His mother asked, "Honey what's the matter?"

The six year old replied, "Mama, Joe just said we're poor. Are we poor? I don't want to be poor. He said those people brought us all that stuff today because we're poor."

Nona hugged the little boy and said, "Those people brought us all that stuff today because that's how they do things in the country. Joe is just not accustomed to living in the country. He's accustomed to living in a city. Do you remember when we lived in the city we exchanged little gifts with our neighbors? It's kinda like that. But, if you're talking about not having any money; then we are poor." She leaned over, kissed his cheek and whispered, "But, we have a lot that's more important than money."

The youngster looked more worried and puzzled than he had before he asked the question. He simply turned, walked away and yelled back over his shoulder, "Well, Joe said he'd just as soon go back to New Orleans. And by the way, I don't like Will Brown and I'm not playing with him anymore. There's something wrong with that boy."

The Kohler parents shook their heads back and forth and mildly laughed.

≈

During the following week, Neb was able to pick up rides into town and managed to work three and a half days on the construction site at the mill. By Friday noon the work was completed and he had earned a few dollars. On his way back to the country, he stopped at a farm and feed store and bought more vegetable seeds and feed for the few farm animals. He arrived at the cabin during the afternoon. Since the days were relatively long, he and the older boys began clearing the piece of land not far from the cabin that Sloan Clemmer had told him he could use. By the time it got dark on Friday night, the plot was ready to plow. Neb and the oldest boys were up at the break of day on Saturday. They hitched the plow behind the mule and began to break the ground. By early evening, the acre plot was plowed, seeded and the garden was completed.

≈

Nona and the boys had spent the week carrying water, washing clothes, cooking, and cleaning in an effort to make the cabin more livable. By Saturday night everyone was exhausted.

Ethel Brown had visited during the week and once again invited them to go to church on Sunday. On Sunday morning everyone was dressed and ready to walk the half-mile to the Clemmer house and the remaining half-mile to the main road to the Methodist Church.

The church was smaller than the Presbyterian Church in size and membership. They saw the Browns there and were introduced to all the other members. Walking back home after the service, they all agreed that they enjoyed going there and that was the church they would attend.

On their walk back home to the cabin after church, they passed the Clemmer house just as the Clemmers were driving in from their church. Nona said that they had all been to the Methodist Church and began to explain the various reasons for having done so. Mrs. Clemmer, who had jumped out of the car to hug all the little boys said, "Oh, I knew you were going to that church this morning. Will Brown came by last week and told me. That little boy tells everything he knows. 'Course, you'll find that out. He's a caution. I meant to get by to see you this week. But I was just too busy. I had to make a new dress for Annie Sue. And, Ruth Ratchford over at the church had a new baby on Wednesday and I had to go over there and cook and help out. You met Ruth last Sunday. Do you remember her? Well she's doing just fine. The Ladies Auxiliary meeting was Thursday and I had to make a cake for that. Myrtle Rhyne was supposed to make it. But bless her heart, she can't cook for squat. You know, I should have invited you to come along. We had a good meeting. Thank goodness my girls help out a lot. I don't know what I'd do without them. Anyhow, I did manage to get Sunday dinner cooked last night and we're expecting y'all to stay. I'm sure glad I caught up with you. So let's just go in and get everything on the table and we'll be ready to eat. Later we can sit on the porch and then we'll have a chance to talk. I think you're going to like the Methodist Church. That's a nice little church. You know it's been there for years. It's as old as our church. Now you little children stay out in the yard and play and we'll call you when it's time to eat."

And, so went the summer. The Kohlers worked, played and went to church. The garden was bountiful. Neb continued to work on various construction sites for John, when work was available. Fortunately the older boys had become adept at farming, taking care of the garden, caring for the animals and various other farm chores. The younger ones had the responsibility of carrying water each day.

There were always necessities that had to be bought. Neb tried to hold back a little money from his salary each week. He and Nona both knew that with winter approaching, they would need coats and shoes. Neb would need them if he was to continue working with John and the boys would need them for school. They would have to walk the mile to the main road to catch the school bus, regardless of the weather. The meager salary Neb earned each week never seemed to be enough. The few clothes the children were wearing were becoming threadbare. There would be no garden in the winter. Several times, after getting off work at a construction site, Neb had gone to some of the mills looking for a job. None of them were hiring.

Nona sensed that even harder times were ahead. In spite of what she had been through and she knew was yet to come, she kept an optimistic, cheerful disposition, especially in front of Neb and the children. In the five or so months since they had come to Gaston, she had maintained a strong front. She had been everyone's source of strength. She had been the leader.

15

Winter came. At first the early fall months made only a slight difference in the lifestyle of the Kohlers. School started and all the boys needed shoes. They had played all summer in their bare feet. Neb had managed to save enough money for the shoes. However, they had left New Orleans without having brought any coats and there was no money left for the coats they would all need later. As the days got shorter and the nights got longer, the cabin seemed darker and drearier. It didn't seem to bother the children too much. Except for Ed, they were all in school a good portion of the day.

Neb noticed that Nona had become quiet. She spent a lot of time pretending to read when she was really just staring at the book. Her positive attitude had become somewhat diminished. He had asked her several times if anything was wrong. She had always insisted that everything was fine.

As the days got colder, the cabin got colder. The extreme weather brought a whole new dimension to the concept of living in a cabin in the country. Neb made arrangements with the owner of a general mercantile to get coats for the boys and himself with only a small down payment. They absolutely had to have them if the boys were going to school and Neb was going to work. Neb wondered if the cold weather or having had to buy the coats on credit was causing Nona to be depressed. Then he remembered that she had become a little quiet before the weather turned really cold or the coats had been bought. He assured himself that Nona would be alright. In all their years of marriage she had always been able to cope with any difficulties they had encountered.

John had continued to have small construction projects around town that kept Neb employed several days a week. Neb arrived home late one evening on an unusually cold night, eager to get by the fire. When he walked into the cabin, Nona was at the cook stove. He immediately saw her red, swollen eyes. He went over to her and spoke.

When she looked up and saw his face and heard his voice, she burst out sobbing. "I'm pregnant." Her body was shaking.

He put his arms around her and quietly assured her, "Now, now, I doubt that. Ed's four years old and you're thirty-nine. I don't think you're pregnant. It must be something else. You'll see."

Still sobbing in his arms, she said, "No, no, I know I'm pregnant." Then, obviously agitated, "I think I've been pregnant enough to know when I'm pregnant."

"Try to calm down. The boys can finish supper. Let's go over and sit by the fire."

She was so distraught. Neb knew he had to do something. "Tell you what; I'm supposed to go to work tomorrow morning for part of the day. I'll ask John to drive me home when we're through with the project. Together, he and I will take you into to town to the doctor and see what we can do to make you feel better."

The next morning after the boys had left for the school bus, Nona got dressed and helped Ed get ready. Just before noon they walked through the woods to the Clemmers' house to wait for their ride.

Of course, Mrs. Clemmer insisted that Ed stay there with her. "There's no need to drag that little boy into town. He'll just sit in that doctor's office and fidget. I hate waiting in the doctor's office. Don't you just hate it? I don't know who they think they are. But I guess there's nothing we can do about that. Sometimes you have to go to the doctor. 'Course, I don't go very much. Out here in the country we usually take care of ourselves."

Nona didn't say anything. She just sat and listened to Mrs. Clemmer and waited for Neb and John to pick her up.

When the two men arrived, Nona got into the car. The three headed back to town. John, in his typical manner, said, "Now, little lady, what the hell's wrong with you?"

Nona managed to smile and say, "I think I'm pregnant, what else."

John as if making a joke, came back with, "Hell Nona, you're not pregnant. You're too damn old."

Nona simply said, "We'll see."

≈

Neb and John sat in the waiting room while Nona visited with the doctor. She finally emerged from the examination room with tears streaming down her face. Neb began to panic. Something must be seriously wrong. He walked over to her, put his arms around her shoulders and asked, "What is it?"

Nona broke down sobbing again, "I'm pregnant."

Neb very kindly said, "Oh, good. I was afraid something was seriously wrong." Whether he meant it or not; or perhaps he was just trying to cheer Nona, he then said, "This is good news. You're going to be just fine." However, it did little to bolster Nona's spirits.

Later on the drive back to the country, John chewed on his cigar and tried to make jokes once again; something he had never done very well. "Damn, I've never seen anything like it. The way you two turn out babies, I'm surprised there are not more Kohlers than there are Smiths." Then, "Oh hell, you've already got so many children, one more is not going to make any difference."

It didn't help, Nona just cried even more. John decided to shut up.

≈

How had the news spread so quickly?

When John stopped the car at the Clemmers' house and Neb and Nona got out to pick up Ed and start their walk back to the cabin, Mrs. Clemmer ran out of the house. "Now Nona if you're pregnant, don't you worry. Everything will be just fine. You are pregnant, aren't you? There's nothing else wrong, is there?"

Nona stood staring at Mrs. Clemmer. She couldn't believe her ears.

Of course, Mrs. Clemmer continued before anyone could say a word. "Yeah, while you were gone, I saw little Ed sitting out here on the porch and he was crying. Before I could get out here to check on him that rascal, Will Brown, ran up. As usual, he was full of piss and vinegar. He asked Ed why was he crying and Ed told him it was because his mama had been crying. Will asked him why had his mama been crying. Ed told him because she thinks she's pregnant. Little Ed said he had heard his mama and daddy talking. Now Nona, try not to worry. It's not good for you in your condition. Go home and lie down and I'll bring supper down later."

Nona said, "Thank you," and turned and walked away. Neb and Ed followed her home. Nona had not meant to seem unappreciative. She realized she was depressed. She would just have to work to overcome it.

Nona's sadness did slightly lessen. At least, she made every effort to overcome it. But it was probably the worst winter she had ever experienced in her life. The weather was bitterly cold. The fireplace and cook stove could not offset the cold air that came in around the doors or through the walls of the cabin. There was very little food in the house, usually nothing more than milk and bread. At Christmas, John came out with a bag of fruit and a small toy for each child. Christmas day was spent around the fire trying to stay warm and reminiscing about past Christmases in New Orleans. There was an old deck of playing cards in the cabin and the family played rummy together. There was nothing anyone could do to make up for the family's predicament. Conditions were not going to change or improve anytime soon. And, Nona was pregnant - a condition she did not welcome.

≈

Finally, on a cold night in February with the help of Sloan Clemmer and John, Neb and Nona made their way into to town to the hospital. It was after eleven o'clock. John went home and left Neb alone in the waiting room during the birth of the baby.

Neb rose when the doctor came into the waiting area. He immediately noticed an unusual look on the doctor's face. Neb instantly became concerned. His memory flashed back to Nona's pregnancies when she was a young girl in New Orleans. She had so many medical problems then.

Before Neb could say anything, the doctor's expression changed to a big grin, "Mr. Kohler, you have a baby girl."

"I have a what?"

"A baby girl."

"Does Nona know yet?"

"No, she's still asleep. I thought you might like to tell her."

≈

Neb was by her bedside when Nona awoke. "We have a baby girl," he said.

"What? I don't believe it." She was surprised, but not particularly excited.

Neb was excited. He stayed at the hospital the rest of the night. When daybreak came he immediately spread the word to all the relatives in town and Emma and Ollie. They all came to the hospital to visit and be a part of the excitement. Everyone had ideas of names for the infant. Neb and Nona certainly had not given any thought to names for a girl. Finally it was decided the baby would be named Daisy Jane, after Neb's oldest sister that had raised him and Nona's mother. Neb then made his way back to the country to tell the boys. Most of them were gone. They had all gotten up that morning and gone to school. Nevette had stayed home to look after Ed, who was too little to stay alone. Neb went into the cabin and said to the two, "Guess what boys, you have a baby sister at the hospital."

Nevette congratulated his father. But five-year-old Ed, disgruntled upon hearing the news, said, "Well, you can just leave her there. We don't need any more people in this house and certainly not a girl."

Of course, the baby was not left at the hospital. It was brought back to the miserable little cabin and the depressing winter continued.

≈

Finally in March, the weather began to break and it was not as cold. The days grew longer and brighter. The new baby stopped crying during the night and waking everyone in the small cabin. The entire family was able to walk to church together again. The boys began, once more, playing with the Clemmer and Brown children down in the hollow.

While Nevette, Elam and Ray were usually busy helping out around the house with chopping wood or various other chores, the other younger children loved to romp outside and make up games to entertain themselves. They enjoyed playing with the Clemmer children more than the Browns. They all thought Will Brown, the younger, was a little obnoxious and Samuel was extremely boastful. Samuel was constantly talking about his good grades in school - even though his grades were not as outstanding as the Kohler boys. Finally when Joe could not abide any more of Samuel's bragging, he said to Samuel, "Look, your grades are not nearly as good as mine and Ray's. So why do you keep talking about it?"

Samuel retorted, "Look, my grades are good enough to get a scholarship to college. Then I'll be able to get out of this place and someday I'll be able to help my daddy. My daddy didn't deserve to get shot. He was a good worker. If he hadn't gotten shot, he'd still be working at the mill. He'd probably be a supervisor by now and we'd be living in town." Then in a slightly angry manner he added, "I've had to work on this little farm because my Daddy can't always. And I'm smart and I can do anything I want."

Whether out of sympathy for Samuel or boredom, Joe decided not to discuss the subject further.

Will, now a teenager, roamed the woods each day; always coming by the Kohler house. Everyone was nice to him, but dreaded seeing him drop by. He was always disruptive and getting in everyone's way. There was little anyone could do to avoid him. So they all tried to ignore him. They enjoyed being able to move freely out of doors once again and had no intentions of allowing Will to spoil their fun.

When the days became warm enough, the garden was planted. Neb and Nona had acquired some canning jars. Some had been given to them and some they had bought. With the help of the children, Nona was able to can a few jars of vegetables for the winter. While not in school, Nevette was working a few days a week helping his Uncle John on construction jobs.

John always said, "I'd rather have Nevette working for me than the sons-of-bitches I used to have."

With the little extra money they made, Neb had made payment on a pig that Sloan Clemmer would butcher and give them in the coming winter. Circumstances did not seem as dire as previously and conditions appeared to be improving, if only during the summer months.

Nona had hoped they would not have to spend another winter in the cabin. The last winter and the birth of another baby had been almost more than she could bear. She knew they had no where to go. There just was not enough money available to even consider looking for another place to live. The most she could hope for was enough food to keep the family fed. She knew they would spend another winter in a horrible state of affairs. But for now they would enjoy the summer months. At least they were not cold and there was a little more food available.

≈

On a hot night in August, the Kohlers went to bed when it got dark. All the doors and windows were open to allow the night breeze to blow through. Nona had not been asleep very long. At first she didn't know what caused her to wake. The baby was not crying. The cabin was quiet. Then she realized there was a glow in the room, far brighter than the full moon would have caused. She got out of bed, walked to the door and looked out. That's when she realized the barn was burning. She called out to Neb and soon the whole family was awake. The flames were already billowing through the roof of the barn.

Starting out the door, Nevette said, "Let's start carrying water from the spring."

As he ran out the door, Neb declared, "There's no use. I think it's too late. The fire's too far gone. I wouldn't want anyone to get hurt. Let's just try to get the cow and mule out and hope it doesn't spread past the barn."

The Clemmers, who had seen the blaze, came down to see if they could help. The girls were still in their bedclothes. As the fire died down and dawn broke, both families stood around the coals and ashes discussing what could possibly have caused the fire.

Neb said, "I don't understand. There had not been a storm or lightening. The children are not allowed to have matches around the barn. Fortunately, there was not a lot in there, only the feed for the animals. We will have to rebuild some kind of shelter for them before winter comes."

"Dan and I will be glad to help you," Sloan Clemmer said. "It won't take much of a structure. As a matter of fact, you can just put the mule in my barn this winter if you want to. I sure am sorry this happened. I just don't understand how it started."

Nona had noticed the boys whispering to each other. She had wondered what they were discussing. She decided not to ask any questions. Instead she finally said, "I'm going up to the house and put on a pot of coffee and make some breakfast. We'll sit down and eat in awhile."

The Clemmers went back to their house and the Kohlers sat down to breakfast together. That's when Nona asked, "Boys, what were you all whispering about this morning down at the barn?"

No one replied.

Neb then spoke up. His voice was stern. "What's going on? Do any of you know anything about that fire?"

"Well," Ray finally said, "We didn't want to say anything because we don't want to pick on him, but Will has been getting cigarettes from somewhere and sneaking around smoking. We know because he has offered them to us." Then in a firm, but kind voice, Ray said, "But, that certainly doesn't mean he started that fire. It would be unjust to assume that."

Roger, who was much younger, immediately in tattle-tail fashion, spoke up, "Well, he was playing in the barn today. I saw him. I know because I left and went somewhere else to play. I told you there's something wrong with that boy."

Neb slammed his fork down on the table. "That little overbearing Will Brown is a rascal. I think I'll . . ."

Before he could continue, Nona interrupted. "Ray's right. We don't know that he started the fire. Boys, have any of you been smoking in the barn?" She then added, "Or anywhere else?"

"No ma'am."

"Neb, do you really think you should do or say anything? The Browns have had enough trouble in their life. That old barn wasn't really worth anything. Sloan Clemmer said he would house the mule this winter. I don't see it as a great loss. Besides, it really wasn't our barn. It belonged to Sloan Clemmer. I think we should all just watch after Will more closely and be thankful that no one got hurt." She paused for a moment and then added, "Boys if you ever do take up smoking, be very careful and don't sneak around."

Neb, who had calmed down, nodded and agreed with Nona. He then added, "I guess Will will always be a problem child. I hate that for the Browns. I wish there was something we could do for him."

The discussion surrounding the barn burning continued as the Kohlers sat together and ate their breakfast. The adhesion that bound the family together was further strengthened. Nona was herself again.

≈

When school started the first week of September, Ed was excited. He would start the first grade. He did not want to stay home another year. And he certainly didn't want to be left there with his little sister - the little sister who had taken away his "baby of the family" status.

Nona instructed the other boys to make sure that Ed was on the school bus each afternoon. This was not a new practice. The boys had looked after each other every afternoon since they had begun riding the bus. When the bus stopped at the main road, they were all supposed to walk straight home. They were to let their mother know that each child was safe and accounted for before they could go outside to play or do their chores. After the crew of boys had been in school for about two weeks, Nona stood in the door of the cabin watching for them to come through the woods and down the path at the proper time. She heard them all running and talking loudly before she saw them. When the boys stepped from the woods into the clearing, she immediately saw what was causing all the commotion.

"Where's Nevette?" she asked.

The little ones, between breaths said, "He wasn't on the bus."

Nona looked in the direction of Ray and Joe.

Joe said, "He didn't get on the bus after school. We looked for him as best we could. Finally, when the bus was leaving, we had to get on it."

Nona thought to herself, *he's old enough to take care of himself. He'll be fine.* Aloud, she said, "I'm sure there's a good reason. He'll be along."

The mother didn't think too much more about it. The boy was a senior in high school and certainly able to take care of himself. The afternoon passed and Neb came in from work. That's when Nona realized it had gotten dark. The family was ready to sit down for supper and Nevette still had not come home. Now she began to worry.

"Neb, Nevette was not on the school bus this afternoon and no one knows where he is. Do you think you should go out and look for him?"

"Yes, I certainly do. I'll walk back up to the main road. I'll also ask the Clemmers and the Browns if they have seen him."

But before Neb could get out the door, Nevette came rushing in. He was totally out of breath from running and trying to talk fast. "I'm sorry I'm late. I hope you didn't worry. Guess what. You'll never guess what." He didn't give anyone a chance to answer. "I got a job. I heard today that Firethorn Mill was hiring. I ran straight over there after school and they gave me a job. I'm sorry I missed the bus. Now we'll have a little more money. Isn't that great?"

Neb and Nona looked at each other, not knowing what to think.

Neb finally said, "No son, it's not great. You can't quit school and go to work. I'm working everyday now and we'll manage. You have to finish school."

"Listen," Nevette said, "After the first half of this school year, there are no more courses for me to take. I've already taken more subjects than I need to graduate. We were all ahead when we moved here from New Orleans. I went back to the school and told the principal I had gotten a job to help my family. He said that after the first part of December, I'll be through with school. Then I'll go back and graduate with my class in June. Isn't that great?"

Nona stepped in the conversation at this time, "That's all fine. But, what happens between now and the first of December? You'll have to go to school during that time."

"Here's the other good part. The job is on the second shift. It's from three in the afternoon until eleven at night. I can go to school each morning. When I get out at two-thirty, I can go to work at the mill at three. I can hitch a ride home at eleven. There's even a city bus that comes part way now."

"Nevette," Nona said, "That's too much for you to try to do."

"Oh no, I'll be fine. School's only five days a week and it's so easy. I can rest on weekends. There aren't as many chores in the winter and it's only for about three months."

Neb and Nona looked at each again. They each nodded reluctantly and together said "Okay."

"Guess what. There's more," Nevette continued. "I've already put our name on the list for a mill house. There's nothing available now and it could take awhile. If we could get a mill house, we'd have electricity, running water and an indoor bathroom. I know it's not like New Orleans. But it's better than this and Mama could get out of the country and this cabin. We all could."

≈

Lying in the bed that night, before he went to sleep, thoughts were racing through Neb's head. He hated the idea of one of his sons having to work in that mill. He remembered how much he had hated it many years ago. Perhaps he should not allow Nevette to work there and try to get a job there himself. But that window of opportunity had probably closed that afternoon. There were still men on the streets looking for jobs. John's business was picking up. He was now working five days a week. Actually the promise of a better paying job in the future was certainly with John and not in the mill. Hopefully Nevette would not have to work there for very long. Neb would not allow himself to believe that a mill house would ever become available. People were desperate. This day and time a house only came open when someone no longer worked at the mill. And that was usually when they died. So for now, his family would spend another winter in a cabin with no electricity or running water – a cabin stuck way back in the woods.

≈

The first winter spent in the cabin was the worst. But the Kohlers would have to endure another winter in that cabin. Nevette was able to get a ride home each night from the mill. A co-worker who lived up on the main road near the Methodist Church had a rickety old car. Nevette had only the one-mile walk to the cabin. It was usually midnight before he got home. But, he got up every morning and went to school. When his school courses ended in December, he had only to go to work at the mill. Christmas came and passed. It was uneventful. The miserable winter finally passed.

≈

The first of June, Nevette was to be graduated from Gaston High School. Neb, Nona and Nevette all wrote to Uncle Elam and invited him to Gaston to attend the graduation. The old gentleman said he would not come at this time. He would wait until there were better living arrangements.

Neb and Nona knew Elam could stay at John's house. Nona asked Neb, "Do you think there may be another reason Uncle Elam doesn't wasn't want to come? Do you think it's his health?"

"I don't know. I surely hope not."

≈

John drove out in his car to take Neb, Nona and the oldest boys to the high school for the graduation. Frances Clemmer walked down to the cabin to stay with the younger children and the baby girl while everyone was at the school. Mary Faye, the oldest Clemmer daughter would sometimes help Nona with the baby. However, on this occasion, she had asked her father to take her to the high school. She claimed she had girlfriends graduating. But everyone knew she wanted to be there to see Nevette. It was becoming no secret that Nevette and Mary Faye were more than just friends.

On the drive to the high school, John continued as he had for years with his off-handed, disparaging remarks about the necessity for an education. "Kids don't need an education. Just look at me. All they need to do is get out and get a job."

"Yes John," Nona said. "We've known for years how you feel about an education. But you can't dampen our day. This is a very happy time for us. I expect Nevette and all the boys will go to college someday. How are you going to feel about that? Oh, and by the way, thanks for the ride." Upon hearing that last statement, John flashed a sideward glance at Nona; wondering if he had heard a sarcastic tone in her voice.

16

Of course, the Kohler family faired better during the summer months. But there were still so many chores that had to be performed. Neb was working for John almost everyday. Nevette was working in the mill. The rest of the boys had to handle all the tasks essential for the cabin, gardening and the animals. Eleven people were surviving in difficult times. The requirements were inexhaustible. But there was always time for church, something the whole family looked forward to each week. Nevette had started going to the Presbyterian Church with the Clemmers. Neb and Nona thought fondly of the Clemmer family and thought Mary Faye was a very nice young lady. Needless to say, everyone knew why Nevette was going there to church. Even Ray thought it was a nice idea.

There was also time for the adults to socialize and the children to play. As usual, the Kohler boys preferred playing with the Clemmers. Will Brown was as contentious as ever. Samuel, who was not going away to college just yet, was still braggadocios. He was working on his father's farm in the mornings. In the afternoons he went into town, where he made deliveries for a grocery store, to earn extra money. He was rarely around and too old to play with most of the children.

However, the occurrence that made the summer of 1940 more memorable than Nevette's high school graduation was the good news the Kohlers received around the first of August. A house in the mill village had become available. Nevette's name was next on the list. That meant the Kohlers could rent it if they wanted to. The rent for the houses was minimal and each family was charged weekly. Most of them had four rooms, small yards and the rent was the same on each of them. Each street on the village usually had one house that was larger than all the others. The larger houses were two-story with four rooms on the main floor and two very large bedrooms on the second floor. The rent was higher on these houses. It was one of these six room mill houses that was offered to the Kohlers for rent.

Neb, Nona and Nevette welcomed the opportunity. Being able to rent that mill house was probably the only way they could get out of the country. It would in no way compare to the lifestyle they had once had in New Orleans. It was in a mill village and there still was not enough money to meet all their needs. But they were thankful for the favorable break. There would be no more walking a mile to catch a school bus in the dark morning hours. The children could walk to the elementary school in the mill village. The junior high school was very close and the high school was about two miles from the house. They all sat at the supper table and talked of electricity, hot water, paved streets and sidewalks. The boys, several of them in their teens, sat and laughed at themselves with statements like, "I never thought I'd be so glad to live in a wood frame house in a mill village." "I really don't mind sharing a bathroom with ten people." "You mean a truck will actually deliver the coal for the coal-burning stove and I won't have to chop wood?" "If I don't carry the water in in buckets, how is it going to get into the house?" "Are we really going to put four double beds in the two upstairs bedrooms for eight boys?" Nona joined in the joking, "Why would I want a washing machine? I've grown accustomed to doing laundry for eleven people by hand."

The move and everything about it was modest, humble and certainly unpretentious. But the Kohlers could not have been happier or more thankful.

On their last Sunday in the country, Mrs. Clemmer orchestrated a picnic at her house and invited all the neighbors, a few people from her Presbyterian Church and most of the members from the little Methodist Church up on the main road. The Kohlers were gracious and appreciated the honor. They were more than polite and promised to come back to the country for visits. But they were so thankful to be moving.

≈

Edison Boulevard was the main artery through Gaston. At the corner of Edison and Scotland Street, a Methodist Church sat diagonally facing both streets. It was a pretty, white wood frame building. The towered vestibule had a set of double doors opening toward each street. The steeple over the vestibule housed a working bell and a loudspeaker for recorded chimes - chimes that could be heard across most of the mill village. It was an active Methodist Church, second only to the First Methodist Church downtown. Its membership would fluctuate between two hundred fifty and three hundred members. There were Sunday and weekday activities for all ages. It was the main gathering place for many families in the community.

The six-room house that was offered for rent to the Kohlers sat beside the church on Scotland Street. The white wood dwelling sat on footings about three feet above the ground. There was a long, narrow porch across the front and a square porch on the back of the house that had a small bathroom. The backyard was the largest on the street. It was big enough for a clothesline, a small garden plot and a chicken coop. The house sat so close to the church, it seemed that the two almost shared a side yard.

On moving day John loaned Neb the truck from a construction site. With so many helping hands, it did not take long to move their few belongings from the cabin and into the house on Scotland. Neb and Nona used the truck to go downtown to a second-rate furniture store and buy a few pieces of furniture, a refrigerator, a cook stove and four iron beds for the two upstairs bedrooms. With Neb and Nevette both working, the store owner was glad to extend credit for the goods. The wood frame house in the mill village and its furnishings were simple. But, everyone was happy to be there.

≈

Of the eleven people who moved that day in August, Nona was probably the happiest of all. The baby was now about two years old and almost self-sufficient. Nona was back in a city - certainly not a large city like New Orleans - but a city. She was able to do so many things she had enjoyed years ago. The entire family became completely involved in the Methodist Church next door, especially Nona. The streetcar ran up and down Edison Boulevard. She only had to walk a hundred or so feet from her front door to catch the east streetcar to the small, downtown business district. She usually shopped at the 5&10 Cent Store for small items like a spool of thread or a nickel bag of candy. But she loved the freedom of once more moving around. She got to know the neighbors immediately. All the mothers were home each day and she enjoyed the almost constant interchange with them. There were enough daylight hours in August and September to sit on the porches and visit in the evenings. Ollie lived two blocks away and Emma only a little farther. They had remained her closest friends through the years. And, they and their families were members at the same Methodist Church. Even though they were both married with half-grown children, they hadn't changed. Emma was still whinny and Ollie was still giggly. If Nona took the west streetcar for a ten cents, four mile ride, she could visit her mother and Ruby. Not only was she out of the log cabin, she was living close to old friends and family.

During the years of the appalling existence in the log cabin, Nona's leadership status in the family had not particularly diminished. But now with this move, it began to flourish. She more than began to emerge. She remained the strong, yet gentle, head of the family and she began to branch out. She became friends, not only with her neighbors, but also with all the church members. Everyone liked knowing Nona and spending time with her. She was a kind person and extremely fair in her dealings with others. Her patient, positive approach would serve her well. She began to take control of so many things that touched her life and delighted in all of them. And everyone who came to know her wanted to be a part of her life.

Friends and church members looked to her for guidance and valued her opinion. By Christmas of 1940, the minister at the church had asked her to become the teacher of the Adult Ladies Sunday School Class, the largest Sunday School class in the church. Until then the minister had been teaching the class. However, he had wanted to lighten his Sunday workload. Finding a qualified teacher for that class was truly a benefit for him.

Everyone was amazed that Nona had the time and energy to take on more responsibility. After all, she had a large family to care for. But she loved the preparation and research that were required for teaching the class. She had learned these skills in New Orleans when she had helped her sons with their studies. She tried each week to make the lesson more interesting than the week before and always interjected a joke or funny story. She displayed a natural ability for public speaking, which only served to make her teachings more engrossing. She enjoyed teaching and did it well.

The seven boys continued to like school and excel in their studies. And like their mother, became leaders. They had learned from their mother's example how to get along with people and befriend almost everyone. They made no distinction between economic backgrounds, social status, upbringing or appearance. They really didn't care about such things and made no judgments in that regard. After all, they had already in their lives been exposed to so many cultures and ways of life. They were able to relate to other students on all levels. They soon became very popular and well liked at school.

The boys participated in all the activities at church and soon took on leadership roles within the youth groups. Rarely were the church doors open for a service, a meeting or any activity, that there was not a Kohler there.

≈

After the Kohlers moved to the mill village, they did not see any of their friends from the country for several months. On a Sunday evening in late October, Neb and Nona were getting ready to go to church for the evening service. The door flew open and Roger, one of the youngest boys, came running in. "Guess what."

Nona said, "Well, I don't know what. And you did go to Youth Fellowship, didn't you?"

"Oh yes, it was fun. But guess what."

Nona started to walk out the door, "Neb and I have to leave for church now. Is there something you want to tell us?"

Roger blurted out, "Samuel and Will Brown were at Youth Fellowship tonight."

Nona turned back around with a puzzled expression, looked at Roger and asked, "What were they doing at our church? They already have a church out in the country."

"Well," Roger said, "I didn't see Samuel. He was with the older boys. But Will said that their church caught fire and burned. There was a storm and lightening and everything. Anyway, all the Browns are going to start coming to church here next Sunday."

Nona looked at Neb and said, "Do you think we should hurry over to the church and speak to Samuel and Will?"

Roger jumped back in the conversation, "They've already gone. They had a ride to town this evening and had to leave to catch their ride back to the country."

Nona slowly said, "I see. Well, it'll be nice seeing Ethel and Sam next Sunday. Maybe we should invite them for dinner after church. Coming Roger?"

≈

The entire Brown family showed up for church the next Sunday. During the service, they were recognized and welcomed by the minister. After the service, they went next door for Sunday dinner at the Kohler house. As soon as the dishes were cleared away, Neb, Nona, Sam and Ethel sat around the table to chat. They had not seen each other for several months and had a lot to talk about. Of course, the first topic of conversation was the fire at the little Methodist Church in the country. Everyone agreed it was sad to have lost the church. But it was nice to see each other again.

It was a pleasant October afternoon. Samuel and the oldest Kohler boys walked around outside and talked. Will and the youngest Kohlers ran and played in the yard and the side yard of the church. The Kohlers kids showed Will the dungeon in the basement of the church. It wasn't really a dungeon. It was a part of the basement that had never been completely finished. Most of the basement of the church had concrete floors and plaster walls. However, there was a portion that was used for the boiler for the furnace. It was like a cave - a big hole carved in the dirt beneath the church - with curving passageways and tunnels.

The youngest Kohlers loved playing there and had explored all the little alcoves and passageways. The side doors to the church were rarely locked and they were free to come and go at will. If the doors accidentally got locked, everyone knew there were keys at the Kohler house. Members might need to go into the church at various times during the week. The organist might need to practice for the Sunday service, someone might want to put fresh flowers on the altar or a member might want to clean a classroom.

≈

By December of that year, when Nona was asked to teach the Adult Ladies Sunday School Class, the Kohler family was totally ensconced in the church.

17

1941

The January morning was cold. The Kohlers woke and discovered freezing rain and sleet had covered everything outside during the night. Neb went into the kitchen and turned on the radio just in time to hear the local newsman announce that all the schools in the county would be closed until further notice.

Nona walked in, still wearing her pajamas. "Did he say there's no school today?"

Neb had started making coffee. He sat the pot on the eye of the stove, chocked the coals from the night before and added several sticks of wood. "Yes, there's some sleet - mostly ice on everything. We're lucky there're no power lines down. John and I had an outside job on that big house we're building in Forest Hills. The brick mason's got a little more work and I was going to start on the outside trim. But, there's no use to even go over there in this weather. Thank goodness, it's dried in." He made a second check of the coffee pot and sat down at the oversized kitchen table beside Nona. "We might as well let the kids sleep late. They'll enjoy that. You know, this afternoon would be a good time to go over to the church and store that stage set from the Christmas pageant. I broke it down and it's sitting in pieces down in the boiler room. It needs to be properly stored somewhere. I think I'll take a couple of the boys with me and we can start on the sheetrock in that new class room downstairs."

Nona sat quietly staring, as if in an early morning fog. She finally got up, poured two cups of coffee, sat back down and passed a cup to Neb. Then she said, "You know Neb, you do a lot for the church, especially with carpentry and manual stuff. You go to the Men's Fellowship Club. But don't you think you might enjoy branching out a bit? After all, we've been going to that church for years now."

"What do you mean?"

"Oh, I don't know. You might enjoy serving on a committee or a board."

Although she still appeared groggy, she was thinking. She finally said, "Oh, I know something that's needed and would be so appropriate for you. Why don't you start a Father-Son Club? It could have some religious teachings. But I think it should consist mostly of fellowship and fun activities."

Neb looked off into space for a moment. "You know, I like the idea. I'd enjoy that and we don't have anything like that at the church. I'll talk to Preacher Gross and see what he thinks. 'Course he won't be over at the church today. I'm sure he won't come out in this weather. I'll catch him later this week and discuss it with him."

≈

By Saturday afternoon the sleet and ice had melted. Rev. Gross parked his car next to the curb on Scotland Street, got out and started walking to the side door of the church. He had come - as he always did on Saturday afternoons - to print the church bulletin for the Sunday morning service.

Seven-year-old Ed was watching from the kitchen window. Every Saturday afternoon he helped Mr. Gross prepare the bulletins. Ed would first turn the crank on the mimeograph machine and then fold all the bulletins, making sure the pre-printed picture was on front. When he saw the car stop, he ran out the door. "Daddy, the preacher's here. I'm going to the church. Were you looking for him?"

Neb followed. He met the preacher in the side yard and walked with him to the church office. Neb sat down and explained his and Nona's idea for a Father-Son Club.

Rev. Gross said, "You know, I think that's a very good idea. We need something like that. I'm sure the Official Board will agree. There's a bit of blank space left in tomorrow's bulletin. I'll go ahead and make a preliminary announcement. Since it'll be a new organization, I'll ask for volunteers to serve as officers. We can meet after prayer meeting Wednesday night and work out the meeting times and details. Of course, you should be an officer – probably president."

Neb nodded. "It would be a privilege. But first we must see how the others feel about that."

≈

Wednesday night prayer meeting was over by eight o'clock. Rev. Gross, Neb and three other men stayed behind to lay the groundwork for the new club. Mr. Jordan, Mr. Cosey and Fred Pearson had volunteered. They all agreed they would hold their first official election of officers after a year when the club was well established. Neb was asked to serve as president until then.

Neb smiled, "It'll be an honor. I guess during the remaining winter months, we should confine our activities to indoor events here at the church. When spring comes, we can have a big event to really kick things off. A picnic would be nice - maybe at the river. Fred, don't you have a river cabin?"

≈

Neb went home that night and told Nona about the meeting and the prospects of a bright future for the organization. "I'm going to serve as president for the first year. We won't be able to do very much the first couple of months until we get things off the ground. I think by spring we should be in full force. As a matter of fact, we're thinking about a picnic down at Fred Pearson's river cabin."

"Oh, that would be really nice. It would be fun for all the sons regardless of age differences. They can swim in the river and dive off the dock. I assume he has a little dock? They can take turns paddling around in his canoe. He does have a canoe down there, doesn't he? I think I heard he has one. And you will need lots of food. You should have a treasury by then to pay for everything. You can cook hamburgers and hot dogs. You'll need a big tub of lemonade. Mrs. Pearson and I can make a couple of cakes. I think all the fathers will enjoy it too. You can make a long afternoon of it."

She talked on, "You know, I like Fred Pearson just fine. But does he seem a little standoffish to you? And just what does he do that he can afford to have a river cabin? I know from helping Flora on the Finance Committee that he signed a pledge card and has a generous offering in his envelope every Sunday." She turned toward Neb and whispered, " 'Course, that's confidential and you mustn't tell anyone that." She continued, "I thought he owned that small hardware store beside Green's Grocery up at the corner shopping area." Then with a question in her voice, "I wouldn't think that small store would be lucrative enough for him to afford a place at the river."

"Well, I certainly don't know about that," Neb said. "But I agree with you. He does seem a little strange at times. John and I tried to do a little business with him. It was just some small stuff – a few pounds of ten penny nails and some sash rope for windows. I ordered the stuff and when I went back the next day to pick it up; he didn't have it. It didn't hold the job up or anything. I just went downtown to the big hardware and got them. But he had the gall to get huffy with me. It kinda pissed me off."

"Now Neb, you just need to put that aside. I hope you won't ever mention that at church."

"Oh no, I wouldn't dare. That would serve no purpose. Besides, I really don't have a problem with the man one way or the other."

≈

Ed was pacing back and forth on the front porch the first Saturday afternoon in May. "Daddy," he yelled. "People are starting to come to the church. I'm going over. I have some old pants to wear swimming. I don't know where Roger is."

Neb looked out the side door and saw several cars parking on Scotland Street. The fathers and sons were arriving for the first big outing of the new organization. He stepped back into the house and picked up the cake Nona had baked. He walked over to the stove where Nona was standing, kissed her hair and said, "We'll probably be off shortly - just as soon as we get everything loaded. There are no lights in that river cabin. So we should be home just after dark. I sure hope everybody has a good time."

Nona patted Neb's shoulder in assurance, "Everyone is going to have a wonderful time. Ed is so excited he's been pacing all morning. The older boys will have a good time too. I'm looking forward to a quiet afternoon with Daisy Jane. Hopefully she'll take a nap."

Rev. Gross had arrived with all the food and a galvanized tub filled with ice. The fathers and sons were arranging all the supplies for the afternoon in the trunks of the six cars they would drive to the river. Neb, Ed, Sam Brown, Samuel and Will got in Fred Pearson's car. The other five cars filled with people in short order and the more than thirty-five fathers and sons began their thirty-minute ride to the river.

Since Fred was the only one in the group who knew the exact location of the cabin, he led the way. They had been riding about thirty minutes when he turned off the curvy, two lane blacktop road onto a bumpy dirt road through the woods. After about one-fourth of a mile, the rough, dirt road ended in a clearing. Fred got out and showed the other drivers where to park their cars. The cabin sat on the side of the clearing. The rest of the clearing was covered with grass that had been mowed and served as a yard for the cabin. The structure was really not a cabin. It was a crudely built, three room frame house with a screen porch. It looked like it was probably built in someone's spare time with used lumber. There were a lot of houses along the river just like it. There were some that were nothing more than fishing shanties. But they were all called river cabins.

Most of the sons could hardly wait to get out of the cars. When they did they started running in circles laughing and yelling, "Where's the river?" "I don't see the river." "I want to get in the water."

Rev. Gross stepped forward and stood in the middle of the group. "Boys, I want all of you to come down to the water with me. We need to understand some rules before anyone gets to go swimming."

The walk to the river was downhill for almost three hundred yards through the woods. When the path ended the trees and brush had been cleared around the dock area. The muddy water in the river rippled against the pilings of the small, splintery dock. A canoe tied alongside swayed gently when the wind blew. Fred's property and dock were situated in a secluded cove. Directly across the cove about a hundred yards was another dock almost identical to Fred's. A family was there, diving from the dock and swimming. Their laughter could be heard across the water as they frolicked and played.

Rev. Gross gathered all the boys around. He spoke mostly to the younger ones and explained several safety rules. After assigning each boy a buddy, he said, "I'm going back up to the cabin and make a tub of lemonade. One of the grown-ups will probably be down in a few minutes and serve as lifeguard. So, jump in and have a good time. Don't get too tired. I don't want to see any sleepy eyes in church tomorrow."

The younger boys dove in first, screaming and yelling as they hit the cold water. The older boys soon followed; each daring the other to go first.

Rev. Gross climbed the hill to the cabin and started making lemonade. Some of the other men began preparing hamburgers. Fred Pearson and Sam Brown were digging a hole in the yard not far from the cabin for a fire. Fred kept a griddle at the cabin that would be placed over the pit to cook the food.

Neb was making slaw. Everyone laughed when he said to Mr. Cosey, "Better let me chop those onions. I'm a better cook than you."

All the men were talking and laughing. The boys down at the river were diving, swimming, playing water tag and taking turns in the canoe. It was hard to tell who was making the most noise and laughing the most – the men up at the cabin or the boys in the water. The older boys came out of the water first and walked to the cabin for a cup of lemonade. Then they hiked around in the woods. Samuel and two of the other boys were trying to find a secluded spot to smoke. And, they wanted to talk about girls without the younger boys around.

About six o'clock Rev. Gross yelled down in the direction of the river. "Come on up boys. Supper's ready."

Ed, one of the youngest of the group, was sitting on the dock shivering. He had been in and out of the water for over three hours. "Boy, I'm glad the food's ready. I'm freezing. I'm going to put my clothes on before I eat."

When the boys reached the cabin, Rev. Gross asked the blessing and the fun and laughter started again.

By seven o'clock all the hamburgers, hot dogs, two cakes and a bucket of lemonade had been consumed. Fred Pearson said, "I guess we'd better start cleaning up. It gets pretty dark down in these trees at night and I only have two lanterns."

Everyone pitched in and helped throw paper plates and cups in the fire pit. Then they began loading the cars with wet bathing suits and pants and the few picnic dishes that needed to be carried back to town.

Fred looked up at the setting sun, waved his hand in the direction of the group and called out, "Tell you what. You five cars go ahead and start back. It's going to be dark soon. I think everyone knows the way back. All we have to do is clean this griddle and dump all the lemon peels. We'll be right behind you."

≈

By seven o'clock that evening Nona had finished the preliminary preparations for Sunday dinner. She picked up her Sunday School book and called to Daisy Jane, "Let's go sit on the front porch. Bring something to play with. I'm going to finish my lesson for tomorrow while we wait for Daddy and the boys to get home from the river." Nona and the little girl settled in on the porch. Daisy Jane sat on the floor and Nona took her usual place in the wooden rocking chair. There was still enough daylight to read and play.

In thirty minutes it began to get dark and Nona was having trouble reading. She sat the book aside and looked up to see the cars rounding the corner at Edison Boulevard onto Scotland Street. The five cars parked on each side of Scotland by the side yard of the church. Men and boys began emerging, still talking and laughing. Nona smiled.

The Kohler boys immediately ran to their home and up to the porch where their mother and sister were sitting. They were all talking at same time. "We had the best time." "Everybody had a good time." "You wouldn't believe how cold that water was." "The food was great." "Boy, we really ate a lot." "Do you think we can ever go again?" "I really like the new group at church."

Nona didn't acknowledge the comments. She looked around and asked, "Where are your father and Ed?"

"Oh, they're coming."

All the cars with men and boys left and went to their homes, except Rev. Gross and his teenage son, J.C. They walked through the yard and onto the porch. The preacher smiled at Nona and said, "Mr. Kohler and Ed will be along shortly. They're right behind us. They were riding with Fred Pearson and had just a few more things to clean up at the cabin. It should only be a few minutes."

He continued, "You know, Mrs. Kohler, you and Mr. Kohler certainly hit a home run when you came up with this idea for a father-son group. Everyone enjoyed it and had a big ol' time. The fellowship was wonderful."

"I'm so glad," Nona said.

J.C. interrupted the two adults, "Dad, it's still early. Jack, Charles, Roger and I want to go to the Youth Center and get a coke. Is that alright?"

Rev. Gross reached into his pocket, pulled out a nickel and handed it to J.C. "Sure", he said. "You'll have to walk home, though. I need to go on to the house."

J.C. was happy with that arrangement. He didn't want his father waiting for him and he loved going to the Youth Center in the mill village on Saturday night. He especially liked going with the Kohler boys. They would stand around and talk. And if they were lucky and had an extra nickel; they might buy a coke for one of the young girls there.

Rev. Gross talked on. "J.C., don't be too late. Remember your mother and sisters have gone to South Carolina visiting family. I've got to preach tomorrow and I don't want to be up late waiting for you to come in."

All the boys hurriedly started down the sidewalk and said, "Oh, we won't be late."

Rev. Gross turned back to Nona, "I'd better get on back to the parsonage. I've got some finishing touches to put on tomorrow's sermon. Thanks again, Mrs. Kohler, for your good idea."

"I'm glad things worked out so well. See you tomorrow. Good night."

Rev. Gross walked back to his car and went home.

≈

Nona took Daisy Jane by the hand, "Come along. It's your bedtime. I wonder where your Daddy and Ed are. They should have been here by now."

Nona tucked the two-year-old in bed, gave her a kiss and said, "I'll be sitting on the porch. I'll be back in just as soon as your father and brother get here." She knew the child would be asleep in minutes. She went back and took her position on the porch.

≈

It was dark now as Nona sat alone on the porch. She kept her eyes on Edison Boulevard watching for car lights to turn the corner. After a few minutes, she saw a car slow down and turn the corner. She stood up and waited. But the car regained its speed and continued down Scotland Street. She sat back down and waited. When she realized she was rocking faster and faster, she got up and went into the house. She checked on the toddler who was sound asleep. She looked at the clock. It was after nine o'clock. She hurried back to the porch and took her position.

She was beginning to worry now. *What if something has happened on that dark, curvy road at night?* She had heard there had been a lot of accidents on that road. *Maybe they are just lost. No, they wouldn't be lost. Fred Pearson is driving and he certainly knows the way.*

She got up, went back into the house and checked the clock again. It was nine-thirty. *What should I do? I have to do something. It's getting late. I know, I'll go next door before the neighbors go to bed. They have a telephone. I'll call Rev. Gross.*

She checked the sleeping little girl once more and left the house. She walked to the neighbor's house and knocked on the door. She asked to use the telephone and called Rev. Gross at the parsonage.

≈

The pastor was sitting at his desk. He had just finished tomorrow's sermon when the phone rang. "Hello."

"Rev. Gross, this is Nona Kohler. Fred Pearson, Neb, Ed and the others aren't back yet. I'm really getting worried. What do you think I should do?"

There was a moment's silence. "I'll be right there."

≈

Nona thanked the neighbors and returned to her porch. In less than ten minutes, Rev Gross pulled up in his car, came to the porch and sat beside Nona. "Mrs. Kohler, I don't know what to think. I can't imagine where they might be. Is there anything I can do for you?"

"I don't know what that would be. I'm afraid they've been in a car accident."

"Let's try not to think like that. I see the boys aren't back from the Youth Center. We'll just wait awhile longer. If they haven't gotten back by the time the boys get in, we'll do something then." The preacher did not want to alarm Nona further. But he said, "Maybe I'll wait here with you and we'll send the boys to the police station to see if there's any word there."

The two waited and Nona rocked faster.

Rev. Gross was the first to finally speak. "Mrs. Kohler, would you like to have a word of prayer?"

She replied, "No offense, preacher – to you or The Good Lord. But, I'd just as soon keep my eyes open and watch for that car to come around the corner."

Rev. Gross reached over and gently patted Nona on the knee, "None taken."

≈

Finally, Nona and the preacher saw car lights on Edison Boulevard. The car slowed and turned the corner onto Scotland Street. It continued to slow down and move to the curb. It was Fred Pearson's car. But, it did not stop at the side yard of the church. It kept rolling and stopped directly in front of the Kohler house.

≈

The men at the river yelled back to Fred. "Are you sure it's okay to leave. We'll be glad to help you finish cleaning. It's been a great day."

"Nah, we're fine here. Go on ahead."

The men and boys jumped into the five cars and the caravan started winding its way up the bumpy, dirt road to the blacktop.

Fred looked around at Neb, Ed, Sam Brown, Samuel and Will. "Let's see men. I guess we need to get that piece of paper over there by the cabin. All those lemon peels need to be thrown into the river. If we dump them out here on the ground, they'll attract critters. Would somebody double check that fire pit and make sure it's cold? I need to give this griddle a good dousing in the river. There's a cake plate over there on the porch that needs to go in the car. Wonder who that belongs to? And whose towel is that hanging on that tree over there? Let's just put it in the car. We'll figure out whose it is when we get back to town. Let's move it before it gets dark."

All the helpers scurried in different directions. Fred picked up the griddle and started down the path through the woods toward the river.

Neb looked around and surveyed the situation. He wondered if anyone had checked the inside of the cabin. He decided he'd do a walk-through and make sure nothing had been left behind. He went inside and checked each room; making sure everything was in order and nothing had been forgotten. He went back outside and picked up the galvanized tub of left-over lemon peels. Night was moving in. He's better get down the hill before it got any later. He started down the path. That's when he realized it was darker in the woods than out in the clearing. He was stepping deliberately and slowly; being careful not to trip over a stump or tree root. He had gone about a hundred yards into the woods when he heard voices. It was not the kind of talking and laughter he had heard all afternoon. It sounded like someone was arguing. *Are the voices in the woods? No, the commotion is coming from the river.* He continued on the path. *Maybe the noise is down at the dock. Fred had said he was going down to the river to wash the griddle. Oh, I know. It's probably someone at the dock across the cove. There was a family playing on that dock earlier in the afternoon. Oh well, it's all quiet now.*

He finally reached the clearing at the dock. He could see better now. In the moonlight it was easy to look around and see the shoreline, the dock and the outline of the dark, muddy water. He walked out onto the rickety dock and tossed the contents of the tub into the water. He took a second look around the area and saw nothing. The only thing happening around there was the sounds of tree frogs and night creatures. He turned and made his way back up the hill toward the cabin.

Neb reached the clearing at the cabin and saw the others standing around waiting. "That looks to be about it. Do you men see anything else we need to do?" On further inspection, he said, "Where's Fred?"

"We thought he was with you," Sam Brown said.

"No, there's no one down at the river. Ed, run in the house and see if he's in there. Will, look in the car and see if he's waiting there."

In moments the two boys returned. "I didn't see him in the house." "He's not in the car."

"Samuel," Neb said, "Go switch those headlights on in the car. Let's get a little light out here and check the edge of the woods."

"Mr. Pearson," Ed and Will began to yell and started toward the woods. Then even louder, "Mr. Pearson."

Neb then said, "Let's just stand still and be quiet and see if we hear anything in the woods." The five got very quiet. There was silence all around them.

Neb had a puzzled look on his face. "This is very strange. I can't imagine where he could be. We'd better find those lanterns and start an all out search through the woods. I hope he hasn't fallen over a stump somewhere. I'm going to turn that car around and shine the lights on the cabin. You all go inside and try to find those lanterns. When you do, I'm going to move the car again and direct the lights toward the woods."

Finally with the lanterns lit and the car lights aimed at the edge of the woods, the five started down the path to the water. They tried to spread out into the woods as they moved along and yelled Fred's name. But the brush and undergrowth were thick and they were not able to walk far from the path. When they reached the river, the glow from the lanterns lit the whole are around the dock.

Ed ran onto the dock and began moseying around. "Look, Daddy. Mr. Pearson tore his shirt."

Neb walked over to the front edge of the dock where Ed was standing. A small, torn piece of fabric matching Fred's shirt was caught on the splintery piling that supported the dock. Neb looked at the scrap of material. He didn't say anything for awhile. Then, sternly he said, "Ed, I want you and Will to go back up and sit in the car. You two boys wait there until I come for you. Be very careful walking back through the woods. We're going keep the lanterns down here. But you should be able to get back up the path with no trouble."

The two boys could hear the gravity in Neb's voice. They instantly turned and started up the path.

Sam Brown spoke, "Neb?"

He answered, "Do you think Fred could be in the water? I'm going in and try to check it out. Bring the lanterns closer – not that they will do much good with this muddy water. But at least I'll know exactly where the piling is."

Sam and Samuel brought the lanterns closer. Neb sat on the edge of the dock and removed his shoes. He slipped into the water; holding onto the jagged piling. He didn't notice the cold temperature. He was more concerned when he realized he could not touch the bottom with his feet. He let go of the piling and allowed his body to sink deeper. His feet immediately touched something hard. He turned his body, grasped the metal object and resurfaced. He caught his breath and tossed the object on the dock where Sam and Samuel were holding the lanterns. It was the griddle.

Half out of the water and holding onto the piling, Neb looked at the two Brown men. "I wonder if Fred could have fallen into the water when he was washing that griddle. I'll have to go back down and check as best I can."

He released his grip on the piling and sank to the bottom once more. It didn't take long. He took two steps in the water and stepped on Fred's body. He shot back up and shrieked, "Oh my God!"

Sam and Samuel stood with the lights looking at Neb. They waited.

Neb was the first to speak. Trying to catch his breath and shake the dripping water that was running down his face, he said, "He's down there. We've got to get him up. It'll take all three of us. Sam, how's your leg tonight?"

"Oh, I can handle water."

"Why don't you two just walk in from the bank and we'll drag him back to the edge."

Sam and his son put the lanterns down and walked into the water. The three men dove to the bottom. They pulled and tugged at the dead man's body until the water was waist deep. They came up, gasping for air. It was easier to move the weight when they were able to stand. They dragged the body ashore. Neb was chilled to his bones. He walked around, got the lanterns and moved the lights closer to the body. The shivering men stood looking down at the sight that lay on the ground. That's when they knew they would not be able to revive Fred Pearson.

Neb removed his shirt. He was wet and the night air in May was cool. He placed his shirt over Fred's head and shoulders. He stood up and spoke with authority. "Now, we need to get the proper officials down here. And I do not want those two little boys out of that car. This is no place for them right now. We're going back up and drive Fred's car to the main road and try to find a telephone."

≈

Thirty minutes later a sheriff's car came down the dirt road carrying a deputy and the county coroner. At almost ten thirty when the officials left with the body; Neb, Ed, Sam Brown, Samuel and Will left in Fred Pearson's car and started up the dirt road to go home. The little boys, who had dozed off earlier in the car, were still asleep.

When they reached the black top and neared the service station where Neb had stopped to call the Sheriff, Neb thought of Nona. *She must be worried sick by now.* The Kohlers did not have a phone. But he should at least call the preacher. The station had closed. He used the payphone on the outside of the building and asked the operator to get Rev. Gross at the Methodist Parsonage. The phone rang for a long time. There was no answer.

≈

Nona and Rev. Gross stood up when the car slowed down on Scotland Street. "Oh, good," the preacher said. "They're home safely. I just hope no one's sick."

The car sat parked at the curb in front of the house for a moment before the doors began to open.

Nona and the preacher had grown accustomed to the dark. And the street light from Edison Boulevard made it easy to recognize the figures that slowly climbed out of the car.

Nona, in a voice just above a whisper, said, "Why is Neb driving? And he's not wearing a shirt. Where's my little boy?"

She started to run down the walk to the street.

Rev. Gross grabbed her shoulders. "Mrs. Kohler, I think you should wait here." He started down the walkway and met Neb walking toward the house.

They said something to each other, turned and rushed to the porch. Neb grabbed Nona and quickly said, "Ed's asleep in the car. He's just fine."

"Where is your shirt?" Nona asked. "And why are your pants wet? What in the world is going on?"

"There was an accident," Neb began. "Fred Pearson is dead. Most of the cars had left the picnic to head home and a few of us were cleaning up. Fred went down to the river to rinse off the griddle and apparently toppled in the water. We didn't know where he was. We looked everywhere around the cabin and woods and finally found him in the river. His body was lodged against a piling on the dock. We pulled him out and called the Sheriff."

"Oh no," Nona said, as she slowly sat back down in her chair. "This is horrible. I'm sorry we ever decided to start this club."

"This is most unfortunate," the preacher said. "But, you can't blame yourself. The same goes for you, Mr. Kohler. The club was and still is a good idea. I hope you won't let this keep you away from church. I just can't understand how he fell in like that. You know he's probably washed that griddle in that river many times. This is certainly a sad ending to a wonderful day."

Rev. Gross stopped talking for a moment. Finally, "Someone should get Ed out of the car and put him to bed. Mr. Kohler, I guess you should get a shirt and some dry pants. If you don't mind, I'd like you to go with me to the Pearson house. I need to speak with Mrs. Pearson. I'm sure she'll probably want to talk to you. Besides, we need to get Fred's car home and you can help me with that. I'll bring you back home later." He shook his head from side to side and woefully said, "It's going to be a long night."

"I think you're right," Neb said. "Nona, I'll get some dry clothes and go with the preacher. Why don't you get Ed out of the car and put him to bed."

Nona stepped off the porch and started down the walkway to the street. "Where are the Browns going?"

"Oh," Neb said, "They're trying to catch the last bus going down Edison tonight. Otherwise they'll have a long walk. They didn't plan to be this late heading home."

Nona left to put Ed to bed. Neb changed clothes and the two men were ready to leave. Nona came back out to the porch. "Rev. Gross, the boys should be back from the Youth Center any minute now. Would you like to have J.C. spend the night here?"

"No, that's not necessary. He can just go on home. He'll be fine. Tell him I'll be late getting in. Let's go Mr. Kohler."

≈

Nona didn't know what time Neb finally got home in the early morning hours. She was asleep. Neb was so exhausted his body ached. He collapsed in the bed. Neither of them woke until the next morning when they heard the chimes from the church playing *What a Friend we have in Jesus*. They went to the kitchen, started the coffee and sat down at the table as usual.

"What time did you get in?" Nona asked.

"I don't know. I didn't even look at the clock. But I know it was after two. Rev. Gross sat with Mrs. Pearson for a long while."

"This must be quite a shock to her," Nona said. "And I don't know how that preacher is going to have the energy to preach today. And I've got a lesson to teach."

Neb wearily said, "I don't think I can face the people at church today. I feel like this is kinda my fault. I started that club and I feel responsible." He added, "I shouldn't have let Fred go down to that water alone in the dark."

"Now Neb, don't go blaming yourself. The preacher still says the club is a good idea. And you can't be feeling guilty over Fred's death. You did all you could. Things happen. You can't control everything. But I do wonder why Fred didn't wash the griddle from the bank. Why did he lean over the edge of the dock like that?"

"I don't know."

≈

Word of Fred's death spread quickly at church that Sunday morning. Nona was able to get through her Sunday School lesson. And Rev. Gross got through his sermon. All the members shook Neb's hand and told him how sorry they were for what had happened and how much they appreciated all he had done.

≈

Back at home after church, Neb, Nona and the boys finished Sunday dinner. They were all beginning to relax a bit. After dinner, the older boys walked to the Youth Center and the younger children found a jump rope and went to the back yard to play. It was a pleasant spring day. Neb and Nona settled in on the front porch for a relaxing afternoon. Between conversation topics Nona would usually read and Neb would chew the end of an unlit cigar until he dozed off.

"Rev. Gross sure did a good job with that sermon this morning. He had to have been really tired," Nona offered.

"Everybody at church was very nice to me," Neb said. "They were all most understanding."

"That's nice," Nona said, as her voice drifted off.

They stopped talking – enjoying the peace and quiet.

But their peaceful, relaxing Sunday afternoon was interrupted when a patrol car turned the corner at Edison Boulevard, came down the street and stopped in front of the house. The Sheriff got out and came up the walkway to the porch. He stood on the top step and looked down at Neb, "Mr. Kohler?"

Neb stood up and shook the Sheriff's hand. "Yes sir, what can I do for you?"

"Well, I guess we need to talk," the Sheriff replied. "Fred Pearson didn't drown. He had been struck on the back of the head."

18

Neb was shocked, "What, I can't believe that."

Nona jumped to her feet, "Who would have done such a thing?"

Neb interrupted, "I didn't notice anything on the back of his head. 'Course I probably wouldn't have. We didn't turn him over. Besides it was dark. I just covered him with my shirt."

"You covered his head?" the Sheriff asked.

"Yes. I took my shirt off and put it over his head and shoulders. A body that's been in the water is not a pretty sight. He stayed like that until the coroner took him away."

Nona reached across and touched Neb on the arm. "Let's just all sit down. Have a seat officer."

The Sheriff pulled a chair around and sat facing Neb and Nona. "Mr. Kohler, the coroner did a quick check on that body last night. That's his job. He found the gash in no time. There was a severe wound on the back of Fred's skull and he could not find any water in his lungs." The Sheriff wiggled in his chair. He then starred into space. He was quiet for a moment. "I need to ask you some questions."

"Sure," Neb replied.

"Did you see anyone around the dock or in the woods when you went down to dump the lemon peels? Or did you see anyone around the cabin or anywhere else except the Browns, Ed and yourself?"

"Not a soul."

"I talked to the Browns this morning. They said they didn't see anything either."

Neb interrupted, "Oh, you were at their house this morning? I guess that's why they were not at church. I had noticed they weren't there. I figured they were exhausted from all that went on yesterday and last night."

"Oh no," the Sheriff said. "That meeting would not have kept them from church. I was out there at seven o'clock. I don't know why they skipped services this morning."

"Hum," Neb uttered.

The officer shifted in his chair again. "Mr. Kohler, I hate to have to bring this up. But some of the people downtown are wondering about you. They say this Father-Son Club was your idea. So was the trip to Fred's cabin. It sure looks like you were the only other person on that dock last night. And now you tell me you removed your shirt and covered his head. And we know you had a little set-to with Fred as recently as a few weeks ago."

Neb tried to stay calm. "How do you know that?"

"Samuel told me this morning. You know he still works part time in Green's Grocery next door to the hardware store. He happened to be passing by when you were there with Fred. He said it sounded like you and Fred were arguing."

"But, I hardly knew Fred Pearson."

"I know that. I also know your respected reputation in this community and I have checked out your background. I don't believe for one minute you struck Fred Pearson. Besides, as far as we know, you had no reason to want Pearson dead."

The Sheriff continued, "Of course, I've also done a little background checking on Fred. Found a few things. They probably don't mean much."

"Well, this is all a strange turn of events," Neb said nervously. "I don't know what to think."

"I wouldn't worry if I were you. Something will turn up. I'd keep this little visit between us. I just felt I needed to talk to you. I hope you understand."

"I appreciate your words. But I hope you figure this out soon."

"Me too," the officer replied. "We have enough to worry about these days. It sure looks like this country's going to get into the war hot and heavy. I've got a son that may have to register for the draft soon."

"Yeah, it's getting messy," Neb said with a worried expression on his face. "We've got eight sons. I'm afraid some of then are going to have to go sooner or later."

"You're probably right. Well, I need to go. I appreciate your time. Try not to worry about this stuff with Fred Pearson."

≈

After the Sheriff left, Neb and Nona continued sitting on the porch.

"This is the damnedest thing I've ever heard of," Neb said. "What could possibly have happened to Fred Pearson?"

Nona was perturbed. "I don't know and I don't care. And try not to curse."

"Neb," Nona immediately asked, "Do you think any of our boys will have to go into military service?"

"The way things are going, I wouldn't be surprised. A year or so ago when Congress and Roosevelt signed that law, the minimum age for the draft was twenty-one. But, from what I hear on the news, I wouldn't be surprised if that age doesn't get lowered – probably to eighteen. That would include several of the boys."

≈

Early the following week after Fred Pearson was laid to rest, Neb and Nona laid to rest their concerns over the incident at the river, Fred's death and the picnic. They came face to face with something far more threatening. The United States had entered World War II. The Selective Service Act now required eighteen year olds to register with their local draft boards. They listened to the news every night on the radio. It became more and more evident that several of their sons would be soon drafted.

≈

Because of their ages and their patriotic convictions the four oldest Kohler boys reported to the Local Draft Board. Nevette, Ray and Joe were classified One-A. Elam was deferred for medical reasons.

Nevette was the first of the three boys to be called into active duty. After basic training, he was assigned to The Army Air Corps. He was sent to Chanute Airfield in Illinois and became a parachute rigger. Nona was relieved knowing that her oldest boy would probably not be leaving the country.

Ray and Joe were called to active duty about three months after Nevette.

Ray, who had scored high on tests given by the army, was assigned to The Signal Corps. Because of his Top Secret Clearance conferment the Kohler parents did not always know his exact location. But in his letters, Ray always assured them that he was in the United States.

When Nona received word of Ray's assignment she said to Neb, "Oh, good. I know Joe will also score high on the tests and maybe he will be able to stay in the country too. Then I won't worry so much about our three children."

Joe did score high on the tests. But fate dictated that he would not stay in the country.

When Nona and Neb received the small letter of thin parchment paper with blue and red stripes around the edges of the envelope, they opened it hoping for good news. They first noticed that it had been written three weeks earlier. They read Joe's handwriting explaining that he was being shipped out immediately to the South Pacific and he did not know when he would be able to send another letter. With thoughts of the attack on Pearl Harbor and the battle of Wake Island still in their minds, the Kohlers now began to worry.

Nona, still holding the letter, sat down at the table and looked up at Neb, "He's already been gone for three weeks. There's so much fighting in the South Pacific. We may never hear from our son again."

Neb sat down beside her. With both his hands he cradled her hand and gently squeezed it. He looked into her eyes and said, "You know, I think they could all be gone for quite awhile. We're going to have to be strong. We'll get our boys back." He thought for a moment. What he said next was either an intended distraction for Nona or a true conviction of his resolve. "Our church has already lost two boys at Pearl Harbor. And there's one boy that just seems to be missing. We have to remember what those parents are going through and be strong for them."

Nona looked at her husband. "Neb, you're exactly right. We could lose more boys from the church. We have to count our blessings and help the other parents as much as we can. I'm going to remember that when I prepare my Sunday School lessons from now on. There are a lot of mothers in my Adult Ladies Sunday School Class who must be sick with worry. Maybe I can do or say something that will help them."

≈

Months passed. Nevette's letters came regularly. He explained his work as a parachute rigger and told how much he missed his family and his steady girlfriend, Mary Faye. "I'll probably never be allowed any time to come home on leave - certainly not anytime soon. We are training Air Corps support personnel here by the hundreds."

Ray's correspondence was sporadic. He remained stationed in the United States. He apologized that he was not allowed to describe his job to anyone. He said, "I'm sorry I can't tell you what I'm doing. My job in the Signal Corps is top secret. I am safe and healthy and expect to stay in this country. Please don't worry if my letters are sometimes late. And please don't worry about me."

Joe's letters were few and far between. Months and months would pass with no word of his location. Neb and Nona would not know if he was in a battle encounter. *Is he well? Is he alive?* Nona waited on the front porch for the mailman each day; hoping to receive a letter from Joe. When, on a rare occasion, the Kohlers did get a letter it had usually been written several months earlier.

Neb always said to Nona, "Well, we know he was alive and safe two or three months ago. If anything happens, the army will let us know." He didn't say that several months during war time can change many things.

Sometimes during the warm summer months when Neb and Nona were sitting on the porch or when Nona was watching for the mailman, she would see the delivery boy from the Western Union Telegraph Office peddling his bicycle down Edison Boulevard. If he turned the corner onto Scotland Street, her heart would rise to her throat. She was so frightened the boy was going to deliver a telegram to her with news she knew she could not bear to read.

As the months passed, Nona kept her Sunday School lessons as positive as she could. There were no young men at the church. They had all been drafted. Almost every mother in Nona's class had at least one boy fighting in the war. Two or three mothers did not have any sons. But they worried no less than anyone else.

Nona tried to remember Neb's words – "We have to be strong for all the other parents." The lesson material for the class was usually taken from a Bible verse. Nona had always been able to apply these readings to everyday living. But it became more and more difficult as the war intensified. What positive could she use?

Each Saturday night she sat at the big, kitchen table with her Bible, books, pencil and paper preparing the lesson for the next morning. Neb was usually starting the food preparation for the Sunday dinner.

On a hot August Saturday night, Neb was peeling potatoes for the potato salad he would make for the next day. Nona was buried in her books. She looked across the table at Neb and stared for a moment.

Neb asked, "What the matter?"

Nona's tone was a desperate plea. "What am I going to say these ladies tomorrow? It's becoming more and more difficult to stay upbeat and optimistic."

Before Neb could answer, they heard the screen door on the front porch slam. Neb was glad he didn't have to answer her question at that moment. Instead, he said, "That's probably Jack and Charles coming in from the Youth Center. They're home early." Louder, he called out, "Hello."

There was no response. Neb and Nona turned and looked at the kitchen door. The hardy recognized the person standing there. They both ran to Nevette as he stood in the doorway. He was thin and pale. The dark circles under his eyes made him look older than his young age.

Nona was the first to grab and hug her son. "What are you doing here? Is something wrong? Why didn't you let us know you were coming home?"

"Son, you look bad," Neb said. "Come over here and sit down."

Nevette slowly walked over and sat at the table. Nona quickly made a glass of iced tea and passed it to Nevette. The parents sat across the table from their son and waited for him to speak.

Nevette sipped his tea and finally began to talk. "I've been sick. The medics at Chanute can't seem to figure out what's wrong with me. There really isn't a decent hospital at that small airfield. My commanding officer was supposed to have written to you. I guess the letter hasn't gotten here yet. At first, they thought I had a really bad cold. But the fever keeps coming back. The chills are really bad. And, I keep losing weight. Since Morris Field in Charlotte is so close by, my orders were to come here and wait. They will send an ambulance as soon as possible to pick me up. You know there's a small hospital at that base."

"Yes, we know that," Nona said. "In the meantime what are we supposed to do for you. Did they say?"

"Not much," Nevette offered. "Just rest, lots of liquids and try to keep the fever down."

Neb spoke up. "We'll fix a place for you down here on the daybed. You don't need to be going up and down the stairs. Besides we can look after you better down here."

The Sunday School lesson and the potato salad did not get finished. Neb and Nona got their oldest son settled in the temporary bed and brought two more glasses of iced tea. Nevette rested well that night. But his condition did not improve.

On Monday afternoon, Ed and Daisy Jane came running from the front porch where they had been playing. Nona was in the kitchen cooking. "Mama, Mama, there's a big brown truck outside with a big red cross painted on the side."

Nona stopped what she was doing and started to the front door just in time to meet the medics on the front porch. They explained that they had come to pick up Nevette and transport him to Morris Field. Nona held the screen door as they came through with their stretcher. Nevette was loaded into the army ambulance.

Nona walked with the two medics to the ambulance. "When will I hear something?" she asked.

The driver replied, "He'll probably be allowed a phone call in a couple of days." He stopped to choose his words. "Or some one will call you."

≈

Nona ran to the phone every time it rang for two days. She had asked the children not to answer it. She wanted to make sure she was the one to receive the call.

On Wednesday afternoon the phone rang. Nona ran, picked up the receiver and said, "Hello."

At first there was silence. She waited. Then the operator said, "I have a long distance call for Mrs. Kohler."

"This is she." She waited again. *Whose voice will I hear? Will it be Nevette's saying he's alright? Will it be a doctor? Or, maybe the Army Department?*

Once again, it was the operator who spoke. "Go ahead, sir."

Nevette's voice was weak and low. "Hey, Mama, I'm going to be alright. I have malaria. The doctors feel sure they can treat it here. It's a real mystery to these folks how I got malaria in Illinois. But I guess I did. They're going to keep me here for a couple of weeks. Then I'll be home on an extended leave."

Nona's eyes were wet with tears as she said, "That's good news. Can you write to us?"

"I should be able to write often. I'll let you know how things are going and when to expect me."

They hung up. Nona could not wait for Neb to get home from work. She sent Roger and Ed to the job site where she knew Neb was working that day. "Go tell your father the good news. I think I'll cook a little something extra for dinner tonight."

≈

Months became years and the war went on. The Kohlers were grateful for every letter they received from their sons serving in the armed forces. Joe's letters continued to be few and far between. Neb and Nona worried about him constantly – not knowing if he was dead or alive. Nona continued to sit on the front porch watching for the mailman or the telegraph boy.

The war began to slow down, especially in Europe. But the fighting went on in the Pacific. The Kohlers rarely received a letter from Joe. Finally in 1945, Japan surrendered. The war was over. The Kohlers had not heard from Joe in four months. When would he be coming home? Was he still alive?

Neb once again assured Nona, "If anything is wrong we would have heard by now."

Finally, on a Monday, a letter came from the War Department. Neb had come home from the job site for lunch. He and Nona looked at the long, white envelope marked "Official." Nona said, "This can't be very bad. Bad news comes in telegrams. It must be good news."

The envelope contained a form letter. It stated that most of Joe's unit had arrived by troop ship in San Diego. After a cross-country bus ride, Joe would arrive back in Gastonia on a Sunday night.

Nona reached for Neb's arm. "This is wonderful. Why he could be home by this Sunday night. That's a good six days from now. That's plenty of time to get here from California."

Neb was grinning. "That's great. Just think; all the boys will be home soon. You know, I think Nevette and Mary Fay will be getting married before too long." He gave Nona a quick hug around the shoulders that she didn't notice. She was reading the letter again. Neb started out the door to go back to work. "Sunday will be here soon. I'll help you cook something special."

Nona didn't look up from the letter. She mouthed, "That's good," and kept reading.

≈

Sunday morning came and the church was filled to capacity. Many of the young men had already come home from the war and were sitting with their proud parents at the eleven o'clock service. Word had spread through the membership that Joe Kohler would be home soon – probably that night. Everyone was overjoyed and had spoken to Neb and Nona. Rev. Gross preached a joyous sermon; giving thanks that so many of the service boys had returned safely.

Nona spoke to Ethel and Sam Brown in the vestibule after the service. "What have you heard from Samuel? Do you expect him home soon?"

"So far we haven't heard a word. But, we expect we will soon. We can't wait to see him," Ethel replied.

"Oh, I hope you hear soon. Having to wait is so frustrating. Well, if you'll excuse me I have to hurry home. Neb and I have so much to do this afternoon to get things ready for Joe. We're pretty sure he'll be home tonight."

≈

It was a hot summer, Sunday afternoon. Back at the house Nona fixed sandwiches, cookies and iced tea for the family. She knew she and Neb had a lot of cooking to do that afternoon. They had planned a big home cooked meal for Joe's return dinner they would serve that night.

After lunch, Nevette went to the country to spend the day with Mary Fay. The other boys went to the tennis courts at the Youth Center. Daisy Jane went out to the front porch to play. Neb and Nona tuned the kitchen radio to Guy Lombardo and started cooking.

At six-thirty Neb said, "I guess I'd better go. I checked on that bus coming from points west and it's due in at seven o'clock. I want to be there to meet him. Daisy Jane can walk with me. We'll be straight home. Do you think you can finish up here?"

"Oh sure," Nona said as she sang along with the radio. "All I have left is setting the table and baking the biscuits."

Neb and the little girl left through the side door. They waved to the people going into the church for the Sunday evening service. They turned the corner onto Edison Boulevard and started walking toward town. They reached the bus station at ten minutes before seven. The evening was still hot. Neb decided they should sit on the long bench outside the building. It would be cooler there. And, he wanted to see Joe the minute he stepped off the bus.

Finally at seven fifteen, the bus pulled into the diagonal parking space directly in front of Neb. He watched as each person got off the bus; hoping the next one would be Joe. When no more passengers came down the steps of the bus, Neb got up, walked to the door, looked inside and spoke to the driver. "Anybody else back there, buddy?"

"Nope, that's it," the driver said.

He took Daisy Jane by the hand. "Come on. Let's go home. Your mama's going to be so disappointed."

They walked back down Edison and turned the corner onto Scotland Street. They could hear Rev. Gross inside delivering his sermon. They walked across the yard and back through the side door into the house.

Neb didn't have to say anything. Nona looked up and saw the expression on Neb's face and said, "He wasn't on that bus, was he?"

"No, it'll probably be next week."

"I know," Nona said. "The letter said it could take a few days to get across country. He'll be here by next week." She didn't know if she was trying to assure herself or Neb.

≈

The following week went slowly for Nona. Finally, when Sunday came, the Kohlers did the same thing as the week before. They went to church on Sunday morning. They told the members that did not already know that Joe had not made it home the week before and that they were certainly expecting him that night. They asked the Browns about Samuel. There had been no word.

That evening Neb and Daisy Jane went to the bus station again. Nona prepared dinner again. And once again, Joe was not on the bus.

When Nona saw her husband and daughter walk through the door that night without Joe, she started crying. "Neb, what if there's been a mistake? That was only a form letter. And, we really haven't heard from Joe. We have no idea where he is. Maybe no one knows. He could be missing or dead."

Neb put his arms around his wife and gently patted her back. "Try not to worry. We'll hear something soon."

But Neb and Nona didn't hear anything. Weeks passed. Word had spread throughout the church membership that the Kohlers were worried about their son. Their absence was noticed each week at the Sunday evening service. Neb walked to the bus station every Sunday night, waited for the bus, watched each person get off and walked back home He'd cross the yard by the church and hear Rev. Gross preaching. He'd go through the side door of the house and shake his head in Nona's direction.

Finally, one Sunday night while Rev. Gross was preaching with all the church windows open, loud voices and laughter were heard next door at the Kohler house. Preacher Gross stopped in the middle of his sermon. He dropped his head and looked down at the lectern for a moment. The commotion continued. He then reached down and slowly closed his Bible. He continued looking down. When he lifted his face and looked out at the congregation, he was smiling. He then said in a voice filled with certainty, "Joe Kohler is home." He raised his arm and hand in the direction of the congregation and pronounced, "God be with you." He stood still for another brief moment, grinned and then said, "I'm going to the Kohler house. I'm sure they'd like it if all of you would join me." He turned and walked out of the pulpit and out through the doors of the church.

≈

It was a joyous occasion. Everyone left church and went next door to the Kohlers. The house and yard were filled with people. Neighbors who were not members of the Methodist church walked down the street and joined in the celebration.

Nona, with total disregard, pushed the special dinner she had prepared to the back of the stove. Neb sent Jack and Charles four blocks down Edison Boulevard to the doughnut shop. It was always open on Sunday nights baking doughnuts for Monday morning. On Rev. Gross' suggestion, Nona sent Ed and Roger next door to the small church kitchen. There was a stock of fruit juices and paper cups kept there for the children in Vacation Bible School. It didn't take Nona long to make gallons of fruit punch. The boys were back with dozens of doughnuts in no time.

Everyone was hugging Joe, especially the young girls. He was thinner than he had been when he left for the service. But, he was still as tall and handsome as ever. His movie star like appearance had always turned the girls' eyes.

By ten o'clock it was time for the guests to leave for their homes. Most of them worked in the mill and had to get up early the next morning. Rev. Gross called everyone to the front porch and yard. He stood on the porch and spoke to the gathering. "Let's all stop for a moment of silent prayer. Let's give thanks for Joe's safe return and thank the Lord for all the boys who have returned safely. Let's remember those who did not make it back. We have one more boy in our church who has not yet returned home. Let's all remember Samuel Brown in our thoughts and pray for his safe return soon."

≈

Neb and Nona spoke to everyone before they left that evening. They thanked each person for dropping by and thinking of Joe and his family. Nona took the Browns aside to chat with them. "I heard at church this morning that there's still no word about Samuel. I'm so sorry. Do you think there's anything you can do to find out where he may be?"

"Well," Ethel said, "We don't really know what to do. We called up to Norfolk. You know that where he first went when he joined up. That was no help. They have no record of him since he shipped out for the South Pacific. We don't know what to do next."

Nona hugged Ethel around the shoulders and said, "Let's us know the minute you hear something and if there's anything we can do."

≈

After everyone had left, the eleven Kohlers sat on the porch until very late that night. The night air was pleasant and there was so much to talk about. Questions were being asked of Joe faster then he could answer. Finally, when Daisy Jane went to sleep lying in Joe's lap, they all decided it was time to go to bed.

≈

The next morning before the rest of the family got up, Neb and Nona sat at the kitchen table. They were still tired from all that had gone on the night before.

Nona spoke first. "Neb, can't you stay home from work today and spend some time with Joe?"

"Well, actually I can. But, I don't think I should. John's got a lot of jobs going on right now. And, I'm serving as foreman on a couple of them. I feel like I need to be there. The construction business has really been good lately."

He continued talking in a pleasant voice. "I don't mind going to work today. I'm so glad to have all our boys home. I don't think anything can bother me today."

"Well, don't leave just yet. There's something I've wanted to ask you for sometime now."

Nona thought for a moment and chose her words carefully. "Have you noticed the Browns lately? It's not my place to say this, but they don't seem very sad that they haven't heard anything from Samuel. I know different people bear their grief differently. But they seem to become distant when I ask about Samuel."

"I've noticed the same thing when we've talked. It's kinda hard to console them."

"Yeah, it's all a little strange. I've thought about talking to Rev. Gross about it. But I've had so much on my mind and so worried about Joe; I just haven't. Besides, I don't want to meddle. I guess we should just forget about it."

Neb drank the last of his coffee, sat the cup on the table and started for the door. "Yeah, I don't know what else to do."

19

In the days and weeks after Joe came home from the service, the Kohler house was busy and always full of people. The family alone filled the house. And there was always company. Friends of the youngest Kohler boys loved being there and quite often spent the night.

Nona didn't know who might come down each morning after having slept on the floor upstairs. She stopped singing. "Good morning, Milton. Would you like a piece of toast or something?"

"No thanks, Mrs. Kohler. I'd better get on home before Mama wonders where I am. 'Course, she really knows where I am. Tell Roger I'll see him later. I think we're going to the Youth Center tonight. I know we're going to the MYF ice cream party at church Friday night." The neighbor boy patted Nona on the shoulder and headed for the door. "Well bye, Mrs. Kohler. See you later." He turned back around and stood in the doorway. "Oh yeah, Mama said if I see you, she'll do the worship center for the ladies circle meeting this week."

Nona shook her head and smiled. She wondered who else might be upstairs. She laughed a soft laugh and mumbled, "I feel like I'm living in Grand Central Station." She started singing again and continued cooking.

≈

Two weeks after Joe got home, the Kohlers drove out to the country for Sunday dinner with the Clemmers. Mrs. Clemmer and Sloan were tickled to see all the boys. After the kitchen was cleaned, the youngest children went to the hollow to play. The older folks sat on the porch and made plans for Nevette's and Mary Faye's wedding.

Ray and Joe explained that they had applied for the G.I. Bill and would be going away to college soon.

"Oh, that's wonderful," Mrs. Clemmer said. "And, Mary Faye told me that Nevette is thinking of getting his license and becoming a contractor. I'm going to love having a house builder in the family. Sloan Clemmer and I can't wait to have a Kohler boy to welcome. I guess Nevette has told you they'll be going to our church. I hope you don't mind if he becomes a Presbyterian. He practically is one already. He's been going there for so long with Mary Faye; it's like he's already a member of our church. Don't you think that little Presbyterian church is pretty place for a wedding? 'Course, the reception will be at my sister's house. It's so nice and very close to the church. Do you really think we have planned enough food? Maybe I should add another ham. What do y'all think? Oh yes, I'd like to have Daisy Jane pass the nuts and mints. I'm going to wear a pink, voile dress. What color dress are you going to wear, Nona? I'll have the florist fix the corsages. Sloan Clemmer has already gotten a new suit. Are you going to get a new suit, Mr. Kohler?"

Neb had been staring off in the distance and not really listening. He sat up in his chair, caught the cigar that almost fell out of his mouth, quickly turned and looked at Mrs. Clemmer. He stuttered and said, "Ah, I'm sorry. I didn't quite get all that. You just let me know what I need to do."

Everyone laughed, including Mrs. Clemmer. She knew - just as everyone else knew –that she always talked a lot.

All the oldest children decided to walk down and check out the old cabin. It was a polite excuse to sneak away. When everyone had left, Nona spoke to Sloan and Mrs. Clemmer. "Have you seen much of the Browns lately?"

"Funny you should ask," Mrs. Clemmer replied. "Sloan Clemmer and I were just talking about that. We don't see much of them anymore. I walked over to their place a week or so ago and took them a cake. I feel so sorry for them. Not hearing anything about their son and all. You'd think they'd hear something now that the war's over. They appreciated the cake. But other than that, they didn't have much to say. And I think Sam looks bad. I don't know if his leg is bothering him or what. He acts like he has something on his mind. I guess he's just worried over his son. I know I would be. I haven't been back since then. I just don't know what to do or say."

"Neb and I have noticed the same things," Nona said. "We don't know what to do to help them. I'm thinking of having a family reunion picnic now that the boys are all home. I need to do that before Ray and Joe go away to college. The weather will be warm for awhile yet. I thought I'd use the side yard of the church. I'm going to ask Emma and Ollie and their families to come. I'm sure John and his kids will come. I'll include Neb's two sisters and their broods. Of course, we'd like for you folks to come. Anyhow, I was thinking of inviting the Browns. But, I don't know if they would really enjoy it. Now just doesn't seem to be a good time for them."

"Well, you just let us know when," Mrs. Clemmer said. She laughed and added, "You know I will bring lots of food."

"Oh, I'm sure there'll be plenty of food," Nona agreed. "Neb, I guess we'd better round everybody up and head back to town."

≈

The next Sunday afternoon after church, the Kohlers started getting ready for the picnic. Nona had also invited Rev. and Mrs.

Gross, their two daughters and J.C. Neb borrowed long tables from the church that Nona covered with white table cloths. The September day was warm and the sky was clear blue. Everyone brought food. It was joyous occasion for the almost fifty people who gathered. It was a celebration of many things. The war was over. The boys were home safely. John's and Neb business was thriving. Nevette was starting his own business and getting married. Ray and Joe would be leaving for college soon.

Rev. Gross approached John and asked, "Now don't you and Neb have a brother out of town somewhere?"

"Oh yes," John replied. He waved the cigar that he held in his right hand. "He lives in Mississippi. Has a huge ranch there. He also takes care of big animals across that part of the state. He's not a vet. But, he is quite skilled in animal husbandry. Nona called long-distance and invited him to come up for a spell. But the son-of-a-bitch said he was too busy right now and just couldn't pull away. Yeah, he's something else – quite the gentleman farmer. The bastard's done well for himself. Neb and I are really proud of him."

Rev. Gross cleared his throat, "Well, that was an interesting insight into your brother. I must say, you certainly have a way with words. I think I'll get another piece of cake."

Aunt Daisy, Neb's oldest sister, had been standing close by listening to John and the preacher. She walked over to where Neb was trying to dip a piece of chocolate pie from the dish. She touched him on the arm causing him to drop the pie for the second time. She laughed and said, "Neb, I think we'd better keep some distance between your preacher and our brother. By the way, what do you hear from Uncle Elam?"

"He's doing well for an old gentleman his age. Nona and I called him last week. He's coming up later in the fall for a week. He'll be here for Nevette's wedding."

"Oh good, I'll get to see him then," Aunt Daisy said, shaking her head up and down.

"Well, you'd better not let him see you nipping that bottle. You know Uncle Elam never took kindly to alcohol."

Aunt Daisy laughed out loud. "Neb, you know I never let anyone see me have a little drink. Besides, it's just for medicinal purposes. Why my doctor even said it's okay."

Neb looked at his oldest sister and smirked.

≈

When Neb got home from work on Monday evening, Nona had more than enough leftovers from the picnic for dinner. After Neb asked the blessing, the eleven Kohlers talked while they ate.

"Nevette, how are the wedding plans coming?" Nona asked.

"Oh, just fine. Mary Faye and Mrs. Clemmer have everything under control."

"That's nice." Looking at Ray and Joe she asked, "Do you boys have everything ready to take to college in Raleigh?"

"Everything's ready to go. We're going to keep working on Uncle John's job sites until the day before we have to leave. We'll have enough money saved by then we won't have to work during the school year."

"Ooh, that's good."

Roger jumped in. "Did y'all hear Uncle John talking to the preacher yesterday? That was funny. And, Aunt Daisy was standing over there laughing. I got so tickled I thought I'd die."

"I don't think it was funny one bit," Jack rebutted. "Uncle John shouldn't cuss so much."

"Well son," Neb said. "I doubt that's going to change. John's been talking like that since he was ten. He doesn't care if it's the preacher or the Pope."

"Did y'all see that hat Aunt Emma had on yesterday?" Ed asked. "That was the silliest thing I've ever seen. Where do she and Aunt Ollie find those hats they wear?"

"Ed, don't you ever let Emma and Ollie hear you say anything like that. It would hurt their feelings," Nona scolded. "They're like family and love you very much."

Charles spoke up. "Does anybody know if J.C. is coming by tonight?"

Before anyone could answer, the telephone rang.

Neb got up and walked to the living room. "Hello."

Everyone around the table kept talking and didn't hear any of the phone conversation. They wouldn't have heard what Neb was saying anyhow. His voice was very low. The call was brief and he returned to the table.

≈

Later that night, sitting on the porch, Nona asked Neb. "By the way, who was on the phone during dinner?"

Neb didn't say anything.

Nona glanced in his direction. "Neb, did you hear me?"

Neb looked around the porch and over his shoulder to make sure he and Nona were alone. "It was the Sheriff. It seems there's been a new development in the Fred Pearson case from years ago. He wants me in his office at ten o'clock tomorrow morning."

"What ever for?"

"I have no idea. I had hoped I'd never have to deal with that again."

"Well, I don't like the sound of this," Nona said thoughtfully.

≈

The next morning Neb arrived at the Sheriff's office promptly at ten o'clock. He walked into the office and shook the Sheriff's hand. "What's this all about?"

Before the Sheriff could answer, Sam Brown stepped into the room. "I asked the Sheriff to call you. I hope you don't mind."

"Neb," the Sheriff said, "Sam requested this meeting. I'm almost as puzzled as you are. He also asked that you be present."

"Neb," Sam said. "I just needed somebody here with me. I couldn't bring Ethel. This is no place for a lady. Will's not a kid anymore. But he sure acts like one. Besides, you're one of the best people I know and I knew I could count on your support."

"Get to the point, Sam," the Sheriff said in a tone of exasperation.

"I can't live with this anymore," Sam said. "My son, Samuel, killed Fred Pearson."

Neb and the Sheriff sat quietly and waited.

Sam's eyes were wet but he continued. "Samuel hit him over the back of the head and pushed him into the river that night. Samuel told his mother and me that next morning after you left the house, Sheriff. I haven't told anybody all these years. I hope you're not going to hold that against me."

"We'll see about that. Go on."

"Well, Samuel joined the Navy right after that and I didn't know what to do. His going to prison would have killed his mother. I decided not to say anything. And now, I don't think he's coming home from that war."

The Sheriff interrupted. "Why would Samuel want to harm Fred? Was it maybe an accident?"

Sam started talking again. "That boy's always been filled with so much resentment. He never got over me getting shot in the leg and having to give up my job. He always wanted to go to college and he never got to do that. He had to stay around and help me out. He was always striking out at something or another. Neb, he was the one that set fire to your barn that night out in the country. He also told me that he set the fire that burned our little Methodist Church out in the country. He just picked a time when there was a storm in the area."

The Sheriff interrupted again. "Sam, I still don't see what all this has to do with Fred Pearson."

"Well, Samuel started working part-time at Green's Grocery when he was in Junior High School. You know, it was next door to Fred Pearson's hardware store. Back then the two businesses shared a telephone party line. You remember, if the other party was talking on the phone you couldn't use your phone at the same time. As a matter of fact, if you picked up your phone, you could hear everything they were saying. No one knew that Samuel would listen in on Fred Pearson's phone calls sometimes. Fred would quite often talk to a couple of men up North."

The Sheriff jumped in again. "Sam, I still don't understand."

"What Samuel learned was that back in 1929 during that big strike at Firethorn, Fred was more than just a union sympathizer. He was more involved in organizing that strike than people ever knew. He played a role behind the scenes that no one ever knew about. He had been asked by these men to stir up trouble amongst the mill hands. He was the one that shot me in the leg. As a matter of fact, Samuel thought that Fred was getting money from those men. I don't know about that. But that's what Samuel thought. And, we all know Fred sure did spend a lot of money."

The room was silent.

Sam shifted in his chair and wiped his eyes. "So, Sheriff, what are you going to do?"

"I don't know." He sat quietly in his chair staring at the floor. He then leaned forward and looked Sam straight in the eye. "Sam, you don't reckon Samuel got off that Navy ship somewhere on the west coast and decided not to come back home? You don't reckon he's hiding out somewhere in this country? You don't reckon you know where he is? Or, you don't reckon you could have been the one that struck Fred Pearson over the head? If you know for sure that Samuel was killed in action in the South Pacific, this would all make a good cover up story."

"Sheriff," Sam said with slow determination, "All I know is that Samuel was on the USS Indianapolis. You heard all about that on the news. There were almost twelve hundred men on that ship. Only about three hundred men survived that mission." Then in a stern, harsh voice, emphasizing each word, "And we don't know where Samuel is." He sank back in his chair exhausted.

The room fell silent once again.

The Sheriff stood up and walked around for a moment. He turned and looked at Sam. "Go on home, Sam. You look awful."

Neb stood up and walked to where Sam was sitting. He laid his hand on Sam's shoulder. "Come on, Sam. Let me take you to my house. Nona should be fixing lunch about now."

20

1957

Jack parked his car in front of the brick house, walked through the living room and into the kitchen where Nona was icing a cake. He gave her a big hug. "Hey Mama, what's the cake for? Can I have a piece?"

"You may not. It's for a meeting at church tonight. But I am cooking a pot of spaghetti with lots of New York Cheese and garlic just like we used to have in New Orleans."

"Ooh, that's my favorite and I can't get it anywhere else. I'm glad I came home."

Inquisitive, Nona said, "I'm glad you came home too, but why are you here? I didn't expect to see you. Don't you have exams soon? That's a long drive from Duke. And aren't you preaching somewhere this weekend?"

"Yes, at a little country church just outside Durham. But I had a little time and I wanted to talk to Daisy Jane and make sure she has everything ready for college."

"I think she does. But you need to talk to her. She's at a committee meeting over at the parsonage right now. She'll be home in time for dinner."

"Are those new kitchen curtains?" Jack asked.

"Oh, yes they are. You know I love this house and everything we did to it when Neb and I built it in '52. Except for those curtains. By the way, he's out in that garden. I think it's too much for him. It's huge. But he loves it and I guess it's a nice hobby. Be sure and make over his tomatoes when he comes in. 'Course, the garden may just be an excuse. What he really likes is having the extra land. And, he can walk over to John's house from here."

≈

"Hey there," Daisy Jane said as she walked into the kitchen. "I saw your car out front. I didn't know you were coming in."

"Well, I wanted to make sure you have everything taken care of for school. Have you heard anything from those little scholarships I told you to apply for?"

"Sure have. I got all three of them. The biggest one is from the Methodist missions program. And, I have already gotten my dorm assignment. It's right next to the one where Mother and I stayed when I went with her to a lady's church conference at that school a couple of years ago. I think everything's done. But you need to go over stuff after dinner. We're having you favorite spaghetti."

"Are you coming to my girlfriend's graduation at Duke next Tuesday morning?" Jack asked.

"Sure am. I'm leaving right after my high school graduation Monday night. You'll have to pick me up at the airport. It'll be kinda late. I got the airplane ticket with money I had saved from babysitting Joe's children. I'm excited. I've never been in a big college coliseum before. You know I didn't get to go with Mother and Daddy when they went to Raleigh for Ray's and Joe's graduation. I guess I was still a little too young then."

Daisy Jane kept talking to Jack. "You know, next fall freshmen can't leave campus for the first six weeks. That's when the new sanctuary at church is going to be dedicated. Will you write a letter to the dean so I can come home for that weekend? Since Charles was chairman of the Building Committee and Mother was also on the committee and Joe designed it, I think they'll let me. Don't you? Do you know the pulpit in that new church sanctuary is almost exactly over the spot where the living room used to be in our old mill house on Scotland Street? Don't you know the members will be glad to have a sanctuary again? They've only had the new Educational Building since Daddy sold them our old house and we moved out here."

"Well, let's worry about next fall when the time comes," Jack said. "Mama, didn't you say Uncle Bascom is coming from Mississippi for a visit sometime this summer?"

"He surely is. Neb and John are planning some kind of family get-together. I'll let you know when. Your aunt Ellie can't come with him though. She's going to stay there to oversee the foremen who help run the ranch."

"What time are we going to eat Mama?" Jack asked. "I've got to drive back to Durham tonight. I've got a lot to do."

"Oh," Nona moaned. "You just got here. You stay too busy these days."

"Well," Daisy Jane commented with a grin. "The way I see it, he just wants to get back to the campus to see his sweetie."

Jack ignored Daisy Jane's teasing and asked. "How's Charles doing since he got his contractor's license?"

"Oh, so-so. He's like his daddy. He builds too fine a house. He thinks that everything should be the best and the best built. You can't make a lot of money doing that. But, he and his wife and two children are doing fine. I'm going to have more grandchildren some day that I can keep up with. Did you know that after the Korean War Ed trained to be a draftsman at that little college over in Belltown. Well, he has started working for an aircraft company in Charlotte. It's a bit of a commute each day. But he loves it. 'Course, that makes for a long day and he doesn't get to see much of his two little boys."

"How's Ray? Is he still working all the time?"

"Oh, yes. They made him president of that lumber company he works for. However, he still spends a lot of time at his church. He teaches the Youth Sunday School Class and serves on several committees. That church also has a building program going on and he's heavily involved in that. And he is doing some kind of work all across the state with the Gideons."

"How's Elam's health?"

"It's okay. He likes working in the mill and has lots of friends there. Did you know he joined one of the community civic organizations? He really enjoys that and never misses a meeting."

Jack thought for a moment. "I know we've all said it before. But we're all very grateful to have had him all these years. We're very proud of him and everything he's been able to do."

Jack kept talking, "Do you have any conference meetings out of town this summer, Mama?"

"As a matter of fact I have two. I'm looking forward to them. I just hope your daddy doesn't decide to make home-made wine again while I'm gone. He did that when Daisy Jane and I went to that last conference. Well, he bottled it too soon. And then he decided to hide it in the closet and it blew up all over my clothes. I don't know why he thought he had to hide it.   Have you ever tried to get sticky, sweet wine out of clothes?"

"Can't say that I have. Can we eat now?"

21

1995

The phone rang at Daisy Jane's home in Charlotte.

"Hello."

"Hey, Daisy Jane. It's Charles. Are you going down to Ed's beach house this weekend?"

"I sure am."

"I thought you and I could fly down together and Ed can pick us up at the beach airport. Roger's going. I think he wants to drive and spend the rest of the week with Ed. But I need to be back in the office by Tuesday morning. I have a Housing Authority meeting and we're also going to open those new apartments for the elderly that we built last year. I asked Elam to come with us. But he has an Optimist event this weekend that he doesn't want to miss."

"Who else is going? Are we the only ones? Will it be just the four of us?"

"Yes, I think so. Everybody else is tied up at church this Sunday. Since we all spent the weekend at Roger's mountain house two weeks ago, they don't feel that they can miss another Sunday so soon."

"You know we were joking that this would be a no-spouse trip."

Charles laughed, "Yeah, we didn't mean it and now it has turned out to be that way. We'll have a big time."

≈

"Ed, I like the new porch rocking chairs," Daisy Jane said as she joined the three men on the deck of the beach house. She placed a tray of snacks on the table between them and asked, "Where are we going for dinner tonight?"

"Oh, I don't know," Ed offered. "We'll worry about that later. I'm sure glad you folks are here. It's been a little lonely since my wife died." Then he joked and added, "And this way we can talk about anybody we want to."

Everybody laughed. Roger chimed in, "Yeah, we get teased a lot and accused of talking about people. I don't think it's really that. We just like to reminisce. I sure wish I could stay all week."

"I thought you were," Ed said disappointed.

"No, I have City Council meeting back in Gaston Wednesday night. I'll have to leave Wednesday morning."

"How much longer do you intend to serve on that council?"

"Just as long as I keep getting elected."

"Well, I don't see how you won that last election. You spent no money on the campaign. And you took a stand on that controversial issue that didn't win you any popularity."

"Well, all that's true, but it was the right thing to do. I'm not going to play political games. And I think deep down all the voters knew that. If I ever have to compromise my convictions, then I guess I'll just lose and that'll be that. You know, Mama always said you should be honest with yourself and do the right thing."

Charles, the most sentimental of all the brothers spoke up. "Do you remember at Mama's funeral in '69 when all the people couldn't get in the church? There were people standing outside on the lawn."

"I guess so," Ed said with assurance. "There were people there from all over that part of the state."

Charles continued, "But the thing I couldn't get over was Daddy dying two years later. You know I took him for all his doctor's visits. He always worried about his heart. The doctor told him repeatedly that there was nothing wrong with his heart. Then he just up and died from a heart attack. I didn't see that coming."

"You know it's said that someone can just pine away," Ed interjected. "I think that's what happened with Daddy after Mama died."

"Well," Charles continued, "You all know when Daddy left Gaston as a young man; he never wanted to go back there. He never really liked the place. But he and Mama managed to raise a fine family there – a family they were always proud of."

Trying to change the subject before her brothers became teary eyed, Daisy Jane said, "Did you know that Nevette is going to be honored by one of the state building associations? I can't remember. How long has he headed up that building inspection department in Gaston? Anyhow, just as soon as he and his wife get back from China the ceremony will be held. It'll be televised and everything."

"We need to all plan to be there," Ed said. "By the way, when is Jack going to retire?"

"Never," Daisy Jane said emphatically. "I think he's going to preach forever. He enjoys it so much. You know, Jack always said his favorite things in life were preaching, sex and ice cream and you have to guess in what order. He's made so many loyal friends in that part of the state. But J.C. has retired from the ministry. They've moved to a house at Lake Junaluska."

No one paid any attention when Roger got up and went into the house at ten o'clock. When he came back out, he set a plate of sandwiches on the table. "I don't think we'll be going anywhere for dinner tonight." He picked up a sandwich and sat back in his rocker. "Has anybody heard from Joe this week?"

"Oh yeah, I have," Charles answered. "He's filling the pulpit at church this Sunday. The preacher is on vacation. Joe's a trained lay-speaker, you know."

"I knew that," Ed said. "But you know I didn't realize until he retired that he was project manager when the company he worked for did that big expansion at the university stadium. Nor did I know that he headed up his company's involvement at EPCOT at Disney World. He never mentioned things like that. He and Ray both did a lot of things they never talked about – at work and at church."

At midnight, Ed brought out bowls of ice cream and passed them to his siblings. "Let me tell you something that happened when I was working at Cape Kennedy on the Apollo Project."

And the four siblings kept talking and rocking.

When the sun began to rise over the ocean, Charles slowly stood up. "Well folks, I think I'm going to bed."

DEDICATION

BY

Daisy Jane Kayler Parish

2008

This book is dedicated to the people who shaped my life. My parents, Neb and Nona Kayler were a true inspiration and beacon.

They raised eight fine men. I have watched these eight men for as long as I can remember. They have been my beacons and my teachers. They have been the guidance and controlling force in my life. They were the ones who raised me.

I always went to them for direction, whether virtuous or practical. Their code of moral values was demonstrated to me and everyone they met by the examples they set and the way they lived their lives daily. I can only hope that I have passed some of what I learned from them to my children.

These eight men who spent so many years in Gastonia touched the lives of many. But they could not have influenced anyone more than me.

They are now all deceased except for Jack and me. My dear Jack played the biggest role in my life. From the time I was born in the dirt floor, log cabin he has always watched over me. He is truly my sweetheart and the love of my life.

The Gaston Gazette,
Wednesday, December 22, 1999

CAROLINA VOICES
By
Jick Garland, Columnist

It's not how you spell your name, but what you do with it that counts

Its astounding to see what one family can contribute to a community. Although they were originally born in North Carolina, Nevette Eugene Kayler and his wife, Nona Allen Kayler, moved to New Orleans in 1916 to enter the ice cream business with an uncle of Mr. Kayler. During the Great Depression, they moved back to North Carolina with their eight children in 1935. Later their ninth child was born in Gastonia. Influenced by their parents, all of the children have contributed to society; however, I would like to put the spotlight on the three of them who served the public sector. Their names and accomplishments are as follows:

■Nevette E. Kaylor Jr. served as chief building inspector in the City of Gastonia from 1966 until January 1, 1987. Upon retirement, he became a part of the Community Development Department of Gastonia and served in that capacity until his death in 1997. He mastered the building codes of Gastonia, Gaston County and the State of North Carolina and fairly and impartially administered them. His decision on any issue was generally accepted because the public realized his competence and impartiality. He was a model for this position throughout the region. He took a great interest in seeing his community move forward, and he eagerly participated in many civic projects and groups.

■Charles R. Kaylor left private industry and began to work for Gaston County in 1965. In 1967 he became the assistant director of the Housing Authority of the City of Gastonia. In 1971 he was promoted to the director of the Gastonia Housing Authority and continued in that position until 1998. He has been very active in the Rotary Club of Gastonia and in many other civic organizations. People in need of public housing had a friend in Charlie Kaylor. He was privileged to serve under an outstanding board of directors composed of leading citizens of the City of Gastonia. He was also recognized throughout the state as a fearless and tireless leader for public housing. Charlie lives in retirement at 1321 Signal Ave., Gastonia, with his wife of 50 years.

■Roger A. Kayler was the longest serving Gastonia city councilman on record. He was in office from 1973 until 1975, from 1979 until 1986, from 1987 until 1992 and from 1993 until 1997. He died on Nov. 15, 1999. He was a fountain of knowledge for the mayor and other council members. He studied every issue carefully and was prepared when the time came to vote. He never failed to vote his convictions even though a majority of those in the audience were on the other side. In 1985 he voted for liquor by the drink. His own family urged him not to become involved on the side of the proponents, but he was convinced in his own mind that he needed to vote for what was best for Gastonia. This vote led to his defeat in the next election. He was a man of strong principles. It will be a long time before another Roger Kayler will come along.

THE ORIGINAL family name appears to have been Kayler. However, the children have divided on which name to use. Six of the children have chosen to use the name Kayler, while three of them have chosen to spell their name Kaylor.

The example set by parents and the discipline which they maintain at home cannot only impact their children but in this case influence the entire community. Children are the byproducts of their heritage. We are grateful that the virtues which Nevette Eugene Kayler and Nona Allen Kayler instilled in their children were the right ones and that the contributions of their children will be with us long after the parents are forgotten.

Gastonia attorney Jick Garland served as the city's mayor from 1987 to 1997.

###

www.ingramcontent.com/pod-product-compliance
Lightning Source LLC
Chambersburg PA
CBHW032143020726
47496CB00003B/696